WL

09 JAN 09,

~~WELL~~

D0262923

Animal Ark™

Pony in the Post
Fox in the Frost

700035194441

a division of Hachette Children's Books

To Toyhorse Wonkytonks
– the smallest horse in Britain

Special thanks to Linda Chapman
Thanks also to C.J. Hall, B.Vet.Med., M.R.C.V.S., for reviewing
the veterinary information contained in this book and to
Tikki Adorian at the Toyhorse Stud, West Sussex, for all her help.

Animal Ark is a registered trademark of Working Partners Limited
Text copyright © 1999 Working Partners Limited
Created by Working Partners Limited, London WC1X 9HH
Original series created by Ben M. Baglio
Illustrations copyright © 1999 Ann Baum

First published as a single volume in Great Britain in 1999
by Hodder Children's Books

This bind-up edition published in 2008 by Hodder Children's Books

The right of Lucy Daniels to be identified as the Author of
the Work has been asserted by her in accordance with the
Copyright, Designs and Patents Act 1988.

1

All rights reserved. Apart from any use permitted under
UK copyright law, this publication may only be reproduced, stored
or transmitted, in any form, or by any means with prior permission
in writing from the publishers or in the case of reprographhic
production in accordance with the terms of licences issued
by the Copyright Licensing Agency and may not be otherwise
circulated in any form of binding or cover other than that
in which it is published and without a similar condition being
imposed on the subsequent purchaser.

All characters in this publication are fictitious and any resemblance
to real persons, living or dead, is purely coincidental.

A Catalogue record for this book is available from the British Library

ISBN 978 0 340 95973 2

Typese   wickshire

T   en's
E   i in
s   the

WORCESTERSHIRE
COUNTY COUNCIL

444		
Bertrams	17/11/2008	
	£6.99	
WL		

LUCY DANIELS

Animal Ark™

Pony in the Post

Illustrations by Ann Baum

One

Mandy put a fresh piece of bedding on the floor of the dog cage she had been cleaning out. 'There we are, Honey,' she said, turning to the golden retriever who was watching her from the cage opposite. 'All ready for you again.'

Every morning, Mandy Hope had the task of cleaning out the cages and feeding the animals that had stayed overnight in the residential unit at her parents' veterinary practice, Animal Ark. Before surgery began, Mr or Mrs Hope would check the animals over and give them any medication they needed. Today there was just Honey.

Mandy encouraged the dog to walk across into the now clean cage. Honey sniffed the bedding and slowly lay down, revealing a shaved stomach with a long row of neat stitches. 'Good dog,' Mandy murmured, crouching down to examine them. Two days ago, Mrs Hope had operated on the golden retriever to remove a large stomach tumour. The skin around the stitches looked pink and swollen and Mandy made a mental note to tell her mum.

Honey gently licked Mandy on the hand. Stroking the dog's silky ears, Mandy glanced at her watch and sighed. She would have loved to stay with Honey for longer but the first patients of the day would be arriving at nine and the surgery still needed to be got ready. Saturday mornings were always busy at Animal Ark. 'I'll be back later,' she promised Honey, as she straightened up and shut the cage door.

Mrs Hope was standing with her back to the sink in the kitchen, finishing a cup of coffee, when Mandy came in. 'Morning, love,' she said with a smile. The sun's rays filtered through the frosty window, picking up the lights in her long red hair. 'How's Honey?'

Mandy explained about the swelling round the stitches.

Mrs Hope looked thoughtful. 'It's probably just a simple allergic reaction,' she said. Draining the last of her coffee she twisted her hair into a knot at the back of her head. 'I'll go and check. Make sure you have some breakfast.' As she left the room she called over her shoulder, 'There are some Christmas cards which came this morning on the table.'

Mandy shoved a piece of bread into the toaster and investigated the cards. *Only two weeks to go until Christmas,* she thought, excitedly. *Only one more week of school!* Most of the cards were from owners of animals who came into Animal Ark. Mandy put them to one side to take into the surgery later and went to the sink to wash her hands. She couldn't wait for Christmas!

Through the window she could see her dad scraping the ice off the windscreen of his Land-rover. Simon, the veterinary nurse, was hurrying up the drive, wrapped in a thick coat and scarf. The toast popped up. Mandy buttered and quickly ate it, tugged a hairbrush through her short, dark blonde hair, and then went through to the surgery, taking the Christmas cards with her.

In the Animal Ark waiting-room, Jean Knox, the receptionist, was just turning on the computer. 'Morning, dear!' she said cheerfully.

'Hi, Jean,' Mandy said, adding the Christmas cards to the notice-board. The surgery was looking very festive. Last weekend she had decorated the walls with red and gold tinsel. She had even put up a tiny artificial Christmas tree behind Jean's desk.

Mrs Hope came in. 'Honey's fine,' she said to Mandy. 'It's just as I thought. Nothing to worry about.'

Mandy was relieved. 'Oh good.' She fetched the mop and had just finished mopping the floor when the door opened and the tall figure of her father came in. 'Has a parcel arrived for me?' he asked, stamping his feet on the mat.

'Dad! Shut the door!' Mandy exclaimed, as cold air flooded into the waiting-room.

'We haven't had any deliveries yet,' Jean said. 'Are you expecting something special?'

Mandy grinned at her and squeezed out the mop in the bucket. 'Dad's ordered a new exercise machine. He's convinced that it's going to help him lose weight.'

'It's a state of the art machine,' Mr Hope said. 'The catalogue assured me that this piece of equipment makes losing weight effortless and easy.'

Mrs Hope looked up from examini red appointments diary. 'If you spend time using this exercise machine as ̣ ̣ ̣ ̣ ̣ ̣ looking through the catalogue and choosing it, you'll lose pounds!' she said, chuckling.

'You can both scoff as much as you like,' Mr Hope said, looking at Mandy and Emily Hope. 'But just you wait, I'll be a new man by the New Year.'

Mandy hugged him. 'Not too new,' she said. 'We love you just the way you are.' She looked at his farm clothes: green padded waistcoat, waxed jacket and sturdy brown shoes. 'Where are you visiting this morning?' she asked.

'Beacon House first and then on to Greystones Farm.'

Mandy was surprised. 'Beacon House? Why are you going there?' Beacon House was a very smart modern house set high above the village. It was owned by a family called the Parker Smythes and as far as she knew, the only animals there were seven-year-old Imogen Parker Smythe's two rabbits – Button and Barney.

Mr Hope looked surprised. 'Didn't I tell you? The Parker Smythes have bought Imogen a pony – an early Christmas present, I think –

and they want me to check it over for them.'

'A pony!' Mandy gasped, staring at him in amazement. 'Imogen Parker Smythe's been given a pony for Christmas and you forgot to tell me! Dad! How *could* you?'

Mr Hope grinned at the expression on her face. 'Sorry.'

'So what's it like? How many hands is it? How old? What colour?' The questions tumbled out. Mandy could hardly imagine anything more exciting than getting a pony.

'Whoa!' exclaimed Mr Hope, laughing and holding up his hands.

'What breed is it? What's it called?'

'Mandy! I don't know. I haven't seen it yet.' Mr Hope shook his head. 'I'll tell you all about it when I get back.'

'But Dad . . .'

'Bye,' he said firmly and, turning, he made an escape before Mandy could ask him anything else.

'Well!' she said, staring after him. 'Fancy not telling me something like that!' She turned to find her mum shaking her head at her. 'What?' Mandy demanded.

'Oh Mandy,' said Mrs Hope, smiling.

Just then the door opened and in came the

first couple of patients. Mrs Hope immediately whisked the first one through to the consulting room and Mandy hurried through to the office to get a white coat. There was no time to stand around talking any more. Morning surgery had begun!

As expected, Saturday morning surgery was very busy. Mandy hurried about fetching things, answering the phone when Jean couldn't, soothing the pets who were waiting, and helping her mum and Simon in the consulting rooms whenever she was needed. She loved having all the different animals to deal with. One minute it was a dog with a cut pad, then an aggressive rabbit and then a cat who was off its food. There was a constant stream of patients.

Halfway through the morning, Mandy came through to reception and found a harassed-looking delivery man standing at the desk. He was wearing a dark navy uniform and was holding a clipboard. 'Well, where shall I put it?' he was saying to Jean.

Jean was trying to talk to him and to a client on the phone at the same time. 'Yes, yes, in a minute,' she said to the delivery man. 'So, you want to make an appointment, Mr Murray?

When would be suitable?' she said into the phone.

'Listen love, I'm in a bit of a rush,' interrupted the man, his face breaking out into beads of perspiration. 'Where do you want this crate putting?'

Jean covered the mouthpiece of the phone. 'Oh, just put it in a corner somewhere,' she said, waving her hand vaguely. 'How about Tuesday afternoon, Mr Murray?'

'But where?' the man persisted, looking round at the three dogs, two cats and a rabbit who, with their owners, were filling the waiting-room.

'Is this Dad's parcel?' Mandy asked, stepping forward. The man nodded. 'You could leave it in the hall,' Mandy suggested. 'I'll show you where it is.'

She was rewarded with a look of immense relief. 'Thanks, love,' the man said.

Mandy watched as he hurried to the van outside and unloaded an enormous wooden crate on to a trolley. He grabbed a brown paper parcel and clipboard from the van, shoved them on top of the crate and brought everything through to the hall. 'Just sign there,' he said to Mandy, fishing a pen out of his pocket and handing her the clipboard. He glanced at the box as she signed. 'It's been very quiet,' he said.

Mandy looked up in surprise. *Quiet? Whatever did he mean?* But before she had a chance to ask, the man had grabbed the clipboard off her. 'Great! Thanks, love!' He hurried out of the door with the trolley.

Mandy shrugged to herself and looked at the crate. It was made of wooden slats and had black bolts on one side. There was a white label on the side nearest to her with two red arrows pointing upwards.

'Mandy! Can you come and help?' Her mother called from the consulting room. Mandy hastened back to work.

The queue in the waiting-room gradually went down. 'Phew!' Mandy said to Jean, as the last patient went in to see Mrs Hope. 'What a busy morning!'

'It's not over yet,' commented Jean, seeing the door open again. But this time it wasn't another patient, it was Mandy's best friend, James, and his Labrador, Blackie.

'Hi!' James gasped as Blackie caught sight of Mandy and bounded towards her. 'Whoa, Blackie!'

'Hi!' laughed Mandy. 'Hi, Blackie!' The dog bounced around her, his tail thwacking against her legs. Leaping up, he put both front paws on the counter, craned forward and tried to lick Jean on the nose.

'Hello, Blackie,' said Jean, hastily backing off from the long pink tongue.

'Blackie! Get down!' exclaimed James, pulling on the lead.

Mandy grinned at him. 'Obedient as ever!'

'*Dis*obedient as ever!' sighed James. He managed to get Blackie under control, then pushed his glasses back up his nose.

Jean started to tidy a pile of papers that Blackie had dislodged with his paws. 'Have you come for anything particular, James?'

James shook his head. 'Just to see Mandy.'

Jean smiled and James immediately went pink. Mandy glared at Jean. She and James were just good friends but he got embarrassed so easily. She hastily changed the subject.

'We've been really busy,' she rattled on, as Jean turned back to the computer. 'There's been loads of animals in. Johnny was in with Brandy and Mrs Platt with Antonia . . .' She broke off as she suddenly remembered the big news. 'Oh yes!' she exclaimed. 'And you'll never guess what!'

'What?' said James.

'Imogen Parker Smythe has got a pony!'

'Gosh,' James said. 'Isn't Imogen a bit young?'

'She's seven,' said Mandy. 'She'll probably need a bit of help looking after it.'

James smiled. 'I can't imagine Mrs Parker Smythe helping to muck out a stable!'

An image of Imogen's mother flashed into Mandy's mind: designer clothes, immaculate make-up, perfect blonde hair, and long pink fingernails. 'Me neither!' she grinned. 'Dad's gone up to Beacon House to check it over. I can't wait for him to come back!'

Just at that moment, the door opened and Mr Hope came in. 'That's what I like to hear, a daughter's enthusiasm for her beloved father to return from a hard morning's work.' His eyes twinkled. 'This eagerness to see me couldn't have anything to do with a certain pony by any chance could it?'

Mandy grinned. 'It might.' She hurried over. 'What's it like?'

Mr Hope thought for a moment. 'Very nice,' he said and then as if that was his last word on the subject he shrugged off his coat. 'Hello there, Blackie,' he said, bending down to stroke the Labrador who was sniffing round him.

'Dad!' Mandy exclaimed in exasperation. 'I

want to know *everything*!'

'All right,' Mr Hope said, his eyes twinkling. 'Anything for a bit of peace. She's a palomino called Star with four white socks. She's thirteen hands high and perfectly sound. She should be an ideal first pony.' He started to look round the room. 'She used to belong to Mrs Parker Smythe's twelve-year-old niece, who has apparently just moved into the village with her mum.'

Jean looked up from the computer. 'Yes. They've moved into Willow Cottage on Walton Road. I saw the removal van there two days ago. I've been meaning to call in and say hello.'

Mr Hope peered behind the desk.

Mandy stared. 'What are you doing, Dad?'

He straightened up. 'Hasn't my parcel been delivered yet?'

Mandy had forgotten all about the box that had been delivered earlier. 'Yes. It's in the hall,' she said.

'Aha!' said Mr Hope, rubbing his hands. 'Effortless weight loss. Easy and enjoyable exercise.' Mandy and James followed him through to the hall. Mr Hope stopped and Mandy saw a look of surprise cross his face. 'It's bigger than I expected!' he said, looking at the enormous wooden crate, half blocking the hallway.

Blackie pulled James over to the box and started frantically sniffing up and down the sides. 'It looks like you open it at the front here,' James said, pointing to the two black bolts. 'This side opens out like a door.' Blackie scratched the wood and whined. 'Stop it, Blackie!' James exclaimed, pulling him away.

Mr Hope frowned at the slatted sides of the box. 'A front-opening wooden box for exercise equipment? That seems a bit strange.' He walked forward to investigate his delivery. 'If I didn't know better I'd say these gaps between the slats were air vents.'

Mandy laughed. 'Since when has exercise equipment needed air vents, Dad?' As she spoke the delivery man's words flashed back to her: It's been very quiet, he had said. Her eyes widened. She dashed across to one of the air vents and peered in.

There in the darkness, something moved.

Mandy staggered back as if she had been shot. 'There's something in there!' she gasped, staring at her dad.

Mr Hope hurried up beside her and peered in too. Meanwhile, James looked at them as if

he thought they'd gone mad. 'There's supposed to be,' he said. 'It's a parcel of exercise equipment.'

Mr Hope started to undo the bolts. 'Well, whatever is in there, it's alive and definitely *not* exercise equipment! Stand back.' He opened the door slightly and stared in. 'Well I never!' he breathed.

Mandy could hardly contain herself. 'What is it, Dad?' she said, trying to peer round him.

Mr Hope opened the door of the box.

There was a moment's pause and then out trotted the tiniest black and white pony that Mandy had ever seen.

Two

The pony stopped and looked round the hall. It was wearing a bright red quilted stable rug. Its head and neck were coal-black but its shoulders were white, splashed with distinctive black spots about the size of a fifty-pence piece. It was no bigger than a large dog. Mandy, James and Mr Hope stared at it in stunned silence.

'It's a pony!' stuttered James at last. He struggled to hang on to Blackie who was desperate to go and make friends with this new animal. 'A pony's been delivered in the post!'

'It's tiny!' gasped Mandy. She had never seen a pony so small. It looked at them curiously, large dark eyes peeping out from beneath an immensely thick, shaggy black forelock. Who are you? it seemed to say.

Mandy couldn't remember coming across anything so adorable in all her life. 'Isn't it sweet!' she breathed, starting to walk cautiously towards it.

'Careful Mandy, it might be scared,' warned Mr Hope. But the pony stepped forward to meet her in a friendly way.

Mandy took hold of its tiny red headcollar. 'There's a good pony,' she soothed, stroking its neck. Its coat had been clipped and the hair felt rough against her hand.

Blackie pulled James over and the two animals sniffed noses. The pony was only a little bit bigger than the Labrador. Blackie jumped backwards into a play bow, his front legs on the ground, his bottom sticking in the air and his tail wagging hard. 'He wants to play!' laughed James.

Mandy turned quickly to her father. 'Where do you think it's come from?'

'Goodness knows.' Mr Hope was investigating the wooden box. 'But this *is* a proper travelling crate. It's got hay, water, straw.' He joined Mandy and James and, after letting the pony sniff at his hands, started expertly checking over its legs for any knocks and bumps. 'Will you take off its rug for me, please, Mandy?' he asked.

There were two straps round the chest and two that crossed over underneath the pony's stomach to keep the rug in place. Mandy quickly undid them and drew the rug back.

'Wow!' James exclaimed. The pony's back and hindquarters were a snowy white covered in large black spots, like the spots on a Dalmatian.

Mr Hope ran his hands over the pony's body, checked its teeth, and then put on the rug again before the pony could get cold. 'Well, he seems no worse the wear for his travels.'

Mandy patted the pony's neck. 'Why's he so small, Dad? Isn't he fully grown yet?'

'Oh, he's fully grown,' said her father. 'Four years old, I'd say, from looking at his teeth.'

Mandy was astonished. 'But he *can't* be fully grown. No pony's this small when it's fully grown.'

Mr Hope nodded. 'Very true, but you see, this,' he stood back, 'is not a pony.'

Mandy stared at him. Had her father gone mad?

Mr Hope smiled at her expression. 'He's a spotted Miniature,' he said as if that explained everything. 'A Miniature horse.'

'Isn't that the same thing as a pony?' James asked, looking confused.

Mr Hope shook his head. 'Miniature horses are bred to look more like very small horses than ponies. Do you see his fine legs and fine head? He's far more like a tiny thoroughbred than a pony.'

A Miniature horse! Mandy looked over the little animal. Yes, she could see it now. Apart from his size, there *was* something more horse-like than pony-like about him.

Mr Hope patted the horse's neck. 'When I was a student, one of the practices that I went to work at were the vets for a stud farm that bred Miniature horses. But I certainly haven't come across any of them in Welford.' He rubbed his beard thoughtfully. 'I've got a book about them somewhere.'

'But why's he been delivered here?' Mandy demanded.

'There has to have been some mix-up,' Mr Hope said. 'He must have been delivered to the wrong address.' He started to examine the box for clues.

James helped. 'Here's the address label!' he called out.

'What does it say?' Mandy asked.

'It's half ripped off,' James replied. 'It has a bit of an address and a name but it's not Animal Ark.'

Mr Hope peered over James's shoulder. 'Miss Tania Bens–' he read out. '16 W–.' He shook his head. 'That's all that's left.'

'Maybe the delivery man dropped your exercise equipment at the house where the horse was supposed to go to and the horse here by mistake,' Mandy suggested.

'Could be,' said Mr Hope.

'Tania Bens-something,' said James thoughtfully. 'I don't know anyone with that name in Welford.'

Mandy looked at the horse and then at her dad. 'What are we going to do with him, Dad?'

Mr Hope scratched his head. 'He should have come with a passport. It will have details of his pedigree and vaccinations and also his owner's address. Did the driver give you anything else, Mandy?'

Mandy remembered the brown paper parcel that had been delivered with the crate. 'That parcel,' she said.

But when Mr Hope opened the parcel, he found that all it contained was a tiny green waterproof rug. Nothing else. 'Hmm,' he said, looking at the horse. 'So, there's no passport.'

Suddenly there was the sound of the hall door opening. 'Let's see this exercise equipment then . . . *oh my goodness*!' It was Mrs Hope coming through from the surgery. She stopped in the doorway and stared open-mouthed at the little horse. Then she looked at Mandy and Adam. 'This may be a silly question but *what* is a Miniature horse doing in our hall?' she asked as the little horse walked forward to meet her.

Mandy explained. 'So, you see, we think the delivery man must have made a mix-up with the parcels,' she finished.

Mrs Hope patted the horse and examined the damaged label. 'Well, I certainly haven't heard of a Tania Bens–. Maybe Jean or Simon will know.'

Jean and Simon were called through and stood wracking their brains for someone in Welford with a name like the partial one on the label.

'It's a mystery,' said Mandy. She grinned at her dad. 'We'll just have to keep him.'

'He *is* very sweet,' said Jean.

'I think I'd better ring the delivery company,'

Mr Hope said hastily. 'They should be able to sort this out.'

As he hurried off, the little horse stamped his front hoof down on the hall carpet. 'Maybe you should walk him round outside, Mandy,' Mrs Hope suggested, opening the front door. Mandy encouraged the little horse out and led him up and down the Animal Ark driveway. James and Blackie walked alongside them.

'Isn't he lovely?' Mandy said to James.

James nodded. 'I still can't believe that he just arrived in a box, though!'

Seeing a clump of grass the horse dragged Mandy towards it and thrust his head down. 'He's stronger than he looks!' she said, laughing. She admired the horse's tiny pricked ears and the pretty black spots on his shoulders. Who did he belong to? She hoped it *was* someone in Welford. It would be so exciting to have a Miniature horse in the village.

Mr Hope opened the front door. 'Well?' Mandy demanded, hurrying over.

Her father scratched his head. 'The delivery office is closed for the weekend. I've left a message on their answer machine but they won't get that until Monday, now.' He looked at the little horse with a frown on his face. 'That leaves us with a problem – what do we do with him until then?'

'He'll have to stay here,' said Mandy quickly.

'But, Mandy . . .' Mrs Hope began, coming out to join them.

Mandy had a feeling she knew what her mum was going to say. Her parents, particularly her mother, had very strict rules about not taking extra animals into Animal Ark. 'We have enough responsibilities as it is to the sick animals who come in,' her mother always said. But surely this was different?

'You've got to let him stay, Mum,' Mandy pleaded. 'After all, where else is he going to go?'

Mrs Hope looked undecided. 'We could take him to the animal sanctuary. After all, we haven't really got the facilities to look after a horse.'

'But he's not a stray,' Mandy objected. 'And the sanctuary is always so busy at this time of year. It's only for today and tomorrow. Don't you think he'll be fine in the garden as he's so small? I could clear out the shed so he's got some shelter.'

Mrs Hope looked at Mr Hope. He shrugged. 'It *is* only till Monday and Mandy's right,

Miniature horses don't need much space. The garden would certainly be big enough.'

Mrs Hope gave in. 'All right,' she said, shaking her head as she looked at Mandy's delighted expression. 'But you'll have to be responsible for him, Mandy.'

'Oh, I will!' Mandy cried. 'I'll look after him really well. And I'll borrow some hay and feed from Susan Collins.' She spun round. 'You'll help, won't you, James?'

James nodded eagerly. 'There's a water bucket and haynet in the crate. We can use those.'

Mandy flung her arms round the little horse's neck and hugged him. 'You're going to be so happy here!' she told him.

The little horse nodded his head up and down. Mandy smiled. It was almost as though he understood.

Mandy and James led the horse into the long back garden at Animal Ark, and tied him to a sturdy tree. They swapped his red stable rug for the waterproof New Zealand rug that had come with him in the parcel. 'This will keep you dry if it rains,' Mandy said, as she kneeled down to do up the buckles at the front. 'And we'll make the shed lovely and warm for you.'

James went to fetch the bits and pieces from the crate and Mandy started to tidy up the garden. She blocked off the section where her three rabbits lived. 'I'll clean you out later this afternoon,' she promised them, as she dragged some packing cases out from the shed to form a barrier. Flopsy, Mopsy and Cottontail hopped happily around in their run, nibbling on the short winter grass.

James returned from fetching the haynet and bucket from the crate, looking excited. 'There's a name on the bucket!' he said, running across the garden and waving a black water bucket at Mandy.

Mandy read out the name painted in neat white letters round the side of the bucket. 'Gabriel.' She looked at the little spotted horse who was grazing on the grass under the tree. 'Do you think that's his name?'

'There's one way to find out,' said James.

'What's that?'

James took a step towards the horse. 'Gabriel!' he called out loudly. The little horse pricked his ears and looked up. Yes, what? he seemed to say.

Mandy grinned. 'Gabriel it is, then!'

It didn't take them long to tidy up the garden

and check that there were no poisonous plants that Gabriel might eat. They untied him and let him loose in the garden as they started to clear out the shed. Mandy carried an armful of tools round to the house and stopped to ring her friend, Susan Collins, to see if they could borrow some hay, straw and pony-nuts. Susan had a pony called Prince and was intrigued to hear about Gabriel. 'He sounds gorgeous! I've always wanted to see a Miniature horse close up.'

'Come round,' Mandy offered.

'OK, I'll get Dad to bring me round later with the hay and stuff. See you then!'

Mandy returned to the shed. Blackie seemed to think he was helping by grabbing buckets and plant pots and racing off at high speed round the garden with them. Gabriel watched him with a bemused expression on his face.

However, at last, even with Blackie's 'help', the shed was empty, clean and dust-free.

'All we need now is the straw, hay and pony-nuts,' said Mandy with a sigh of relief as she carried the last of the garden tools into the house and put them on some plastic sheeting in the study.

James followed her through into the kitchen and collapsed into a chair. He ran a hand through his hair, making it stick up in all directions. 'My arms ache!'

'Mine too!' Mandy agreed, as she took down a couple of glasses from the pine cupboard. 'Do you want some lemonade?'

As James nodded, the door opened and Mr Hope popped his head round. 'I thought I heard you come in,' he said. 'I found this and thought you might be interested in it.' He handed a book to James. 'See you later, I'm off out.'

James read out the title of the book as the door shut behind Mr Hope. '*The Miniature horse* by L. M. Redmond.'

Mandy put two glasses of lemonade and the biscuit tin on the table and sat down beside him. 'What does it say?'

'Lots,' said James, flicking through the pages. He stopped on a page that showed a picture of two Miniature horses pulling a trap and a picture of a child riding a Miniature horse. 'Look, they can be ridden.'

'By very small children,' said Mandy.

James helped himself to a ginger biscuit and turned to a chapter called 'Care of the Miniature horse'. 'It says here that Miniature horses can easily be kept on a small plot of land providing they have regular exercise.' He looked up. 'We'll have to take Gabriel for a walk tomorrow.'

Mandy nodded. That sounded like a brilliant idea. She imagined walking through the village with Gabriel at her side. How people would stare! She heard the sound of a car outside and looked out through the window. It was Susan and her dad. Draining the last of her lemonade Mandy went to open the front door. 'Hi!' she called to them. 'Come and see him. He's round the back.'

Susan was enchanted with the little horse. 'He's tiny!' she said as he came over and nuzzled their hands. She fed him a few pony-nuts which he gobbled up in no time, pushing against her pockets to see if there were any more.

'He's in really good condition,' Mandy said. 'I just wish we knew who he belonged to.'

'I can't think of anyone called Tania in Welford,' said Susan. Gabriel pushed his head against her, demanding attention. Susan smiled. 'I'd like a Miniature horse. I'm sure Prince would like the company.'

'Oh no,' Mr Collins said hastily. 'One horse is *quite* enough.' He moved away from Gabriel. 'Come on, I think we'd better get that hay and straw unloaded from the car.'

Mandy and James helped carry the hay, straw and pony-nuts round to the garden. Susan had also brought them some old grooming brushes of Prince's. 'It's really kind of you. Thanks,' said Mandy.

'No problem,' said Susan, getting into the car. 'Why don't you walk him round to my house tomorrow? I'm sure Prince would love to meet him.'

'That's a great idea!' said Mandy, looking at James who nodded enthusiastically. 'See you tomorrow then!'

Mandy and James put down a bed of straw in the shed, filled the haynet and gave Gabriel a couple of handfuls of pony-nuts in a bucket and then James helped Mandy to clean out Flopsy, Mopsy and Cottontail.

As Mandy lifted the rabbits back into their hutches, James looked at his watch. 'I'd better go. Mum will be wondering where I am.' They arranged to meet at nine-thirty the next morning and then James cycled off with Blackie trotting alongside.

Mandy woke up the next morning with a feeling that something exciting had happened. She lay in bed for a moment and then suddenly shot bolt upright as she remembered. Of course! *Gabriel!* She threw back her duvet and raced to the window. The little horse was grazing peacefully in the early morning light. His head was down, his rug slightly askew.

After hurriedly dressing, Mandy ran down the stairs, opened the patio windows and went out.

'Gabriel!' she called softly.

The little horse looked up and then, with a gentle whicker of recognition, walked towards her. 'Good morning,' she murmured as he reached her. She stroked his neck. 'Do you want some breakfast?'

It didn't take long to feed Gabriel and straighten his rug. Then, leaving him to graze in peace, Mandy hurried round to the residential wing to tend to Honey the golden retriever.

James arrived after breakfast. They groomed Gabriel, cleaned out the shed, and then took him out for a walk towards Susan Collins's house on Walton Road. As they walked through the village, Blackie on one side of them, Gabriel on the other, they drew quite a lot of attention. Everyone they walked past wanted to stop and pat Gabriel and ask questions. The little horse seemed only too happy to be fussed over, nuzzling them and nibbling their pockets. I like this place, his dark eyes seemed to say happily.

'I think Jean said that that's the house that Imogen Parker Smythe's cousin has moved into,' Mandy said, as she and James approached a small stone house with a sign outside saying Willow Cottage. It had a small square front garden and a path that led round to a garden at the back. There were some wooden packing cases and two chairs outside.

'It would be strange having Imogen Parker Smythe as your cousin, wouldn't it?' said James as they walked Blackie and Gabriel past. 'I mean, living in a normal house like this and having a cousin with a mansion with stables, tennis court, helicopter pad . . .'

'Swimming-pool,' added Mandy. 'Yes, very strange.' Her eyes suddenly caught sight of a girl looking out of an upstairs window. She was staring at them. Mandy nudged James. 'Look!' she said, smiling and raising her hand to wave at the girl. 'That must be . . .' Her voice trailed off as the face withdrew abruptly and the curtains were pulled sharply across.

'Oh,' Mandy said.

James frowned. 'That was a bit odd.'

Mandy nodded. 'Weird.' She thought about it for a moment and then shrugged. 'Oh well, never mind. Maybe she didn't see us.' She patted Gabriel's neck. 'Come on, let's try a trot!'

With Blackie bounding alongside James, and Gabriel pulling at the leadrope, they charged up the road.

Three

After filling up Gabriel's evening water bucket and shaking out some more straw on to his bed in the shed, Mandy sat in a chair on the patio and watched him grazing his way slowly round the garden. She dug her hands deep into her pockets. It was cold but she wanted to make the most of every minute of having Gabriel in the garden.

The little horse's teeth made a rhythmical tearing, chewing sound as he ripped up the grass. His ears twitched and his tiny hooves stamped into the lawn.

Whose horse are you? Mandy thought as she watched him work his way nearer and nearer to where she was sitting. 'Good boy,' she murmured as the little horse reached the edge of the patio. Daintily, he stepped on to the patio and walked right up to her. She reached out to stroke him and he nuzzled at her hair. She giggled and ducked. 'It's my hair, Gabriel! Not hay!'

'An easy mistake,' Mrs Hope said, coming out of the house and on to the patio. She ruffled Mandy's untidy blonde hair and patted Gabriel's neck. 'He's adorable, isn't he?'

Mandy grinned. 'And so friendly.'

'Miniature horses normally are,' said Mrs Hope. 'They love people and they make great companions.'

Gabriel wandered back on to the grass and for a while they both watched him. Then Mandy sighed and turned to Mrs Hope. 'Where do you think he's come from, Mum? And who do you think he's supposed to have been going to?'

Mrs Hope put her hand gently round Mandy's shoulders. 'I guess we'll find out tomorrow.'

Mandy nodded and looked at Gabriel. Yes, Mum was right. Tomorrow they would find out.

The delivery office was still not open when Mandy set off for school the next morning. 'I'll ring them later,' Mr Hope promised her. 'And then we should be able to sort out this mix-up.'

Mandy went round to the garden. 'Bye, Gabe,' she whispered, kissing his soft nose. He tickled her cheek with his lips and she felt her heart twist at the thought that he might not be there when she got home.

Mrs Hope opened the patio windows. 'Mandy! You'll be late.'

With one last look at Gabriel, Mandy got on her bike and cycled through the village to the Fox and Goose crossroads to meet James. He wasn't there. She stopped her bike by the kerb and waited. Her mind was full of thoughts of Gabriel. Who was this Tania Bens-something who owned him and where did she live?

'Mandy!' A voice broke into her thoughts. A boy came hurrying towards her out of the Fox and Goose pub.

'John!' she said in surprise. 'Hi! I didn't know you were home.'

'We broke up on Friday,' John Hardy said. 'Dad collected me on Saturday. That's the good thing about boarding-school, longer holidays!'

John went to a boarding-school in the Lake District. Mandy had first become friendly with him a couple of holidays ago. 'How are Button and Barney?' she asked. 'Have you got them at the moment or has Imogen?'

'I have. Dad and I collected them yesterday.' Button and Barney were two rabbits that John shared with Imogen Parker Smythe. John looked after them in the holidays whenever Imogen was away and Imogen looked after them in term-time when John was at school. Mandy thought it was a very good deal because it meant that the two rabbits got lots of love and attention all the time.

'You'll have to come and see them,' John told her, pushing a hand through his dark hair. 'I'm having them *all* holiday.' His eyes shone with pleasure. 'Imogen's got a new pony and she's going to be busy with that for the next few weeks.'

'Oh yes!' In the excitement of having Gabriel to stay Mandy had virtually forgotten about Star, Imogen's new pony. 'Have you seen the pony?'

'Just briefly,' said John. He shrugged dismissively. 'It was sort of gold-coloured.' He returned to a subject that interested him far more. 'You should see how much Button and Barney have grown. I'm going to make each of them up a little stocking with rabbit treats for Christmas. You *must* come and see them.'

'I will,' promised Mandy. She saw James cycling at breakneck speed towards them and got back on her bike. 'I'd better go or we'll be late for school. *Some* of us haven't broken up yet. I'll ring you when we have. Only another five days to go!'

James screeched up behind her as she started off. 'Sorry, Mandy!' he gasped, pushing his glasses back up his nose. 'I overslept!'

'What's new?' Mandy grinned. 'Come on, I'll race you up the hill.'

Once at school, Mandy and James went to their separate classes. 'See you later!' Mandy called, hitching her bag on to her shoulder. Miss Potter, her class teacher, hated anyone being late.

But today it was Miss Potter who was late. 'You're lucky!' Susan Collins said, looking at the clock as Mandy thankfully sat down at the desk next to her. 'How's Gabriel?' But before Mandy could answer, Miss Potter came into the classroom. With her was a girl with blonde hair whom Mandy didn't recognise. The girl glanced quickly round the class and then dropped her eyes to the floor.

There was a hasty shuffling of chairs and the sound of desk lids closing. 'Good morning, class!' said Miss Potter, putting her bag down on the desk and adjusting her large, round glasses.

'Good morning, Miss Potter,' the class replied. Mandy looked curiously at the girl. Who was she? Her shoulder-length hair fell like a curtain across her face.

Miss Potter smiled round at the class. 'Well, everyone, I would like you to meet your new classmate, Tania Benster.'

Mandy almost jumped out of her seat in surprise. *Tania Benster!* Just like the name on Gabriel's crate!

'Tania will be starting school with us after Christmas,' continued Miss Potter, 'and so she is going to spend this week getting to know you all and getting to know the school.' She pointed to an empty desk behind Mandy. 'If you'd like to take that spare seat there, Tania.'

Tania walked down the row of desks. The people she passed looked curiously at her but she stared at the floor, not meeting their eyes. Reaching the empty place she sat down.

Mandy swung eagerly round in her seat. 'Do you . . .?'

'No talking, please, Mandy,' Miss Potter interrupted, her voice firm. 'Turn round. I want to take the register. You'll have plenty of time to get to know Tania later.'

Mandy had to sit through the register, almost bursting with excitement. She was longing to ask Tania about Gabriel. Was she his owner? Unable to resist a quick glance over her shoulder, Mandy saw that the new girl had taken a notebook out and was drawing on the cover. Mandy craned round further to see what she was drawing. It was a horse! At that moment, Tania looked up. Seeing Mandy watching her she quickly covered her drawing with her arm.

Mandy was about to whisper something when Susan nudged her. Miss Potter had just read out Mandy's name for the second time. 'Here, Miss Potter!' Mandy said, swinging round hastily to face the front.

Miss Potter finished the register and gave out some notices and then the bell for Assembly went. The instant Miss Potter told them to line up, Mandy seized her chance. 'Hi!' she said excitedly to Tania. 'I'm Mandy Hope. I live at the vets in Welford. Were you expecting a Miniature horse to arrive on Saturday?' Not waiting for Tania to answer Mandy raced on. 'Well, he was delivered to us instead! He had a label on his box that said "Miss Tania Bens–"

but we didn't know who that was so we kept him until we could get in touch with the delivery people. He's so sweet!'

Gradually it began to filter through to her that Tania was just staring at her, not saying a word. 'He *is* yours, isn't he?' Mandy asked.

Tania drew back. 'No . . . no,' she stammered, her face pale.

Mandy stared at her in surprise. 'But he's got to be!'

'He's not!' Tania looked around the fast-emptying classroom as if she was trying to find a way to escape. 'I . . . I don't know what you're talking about.'

Mandy could hardly believe her ears. 'But it said on the box, Tania Bens-something. Isn't that you?'

'No!' Tania exclaimed, jumping to her feet. 'I told you, he's not mine! I hate horses! All of them. Now just leave me alone, will you!' Pushing past Mandy, she ran out of the classroom.

Mandy stared after her in astonishment.

'Well!' said Susan, who was standing beside Mandy. 'What was all *that* about?'

'I don't know,' Mandy said, as they hurried out of the classroom and down the corridor. 'I only asked if Gabriel was hers.' She was taken aback by Tania's abruptness and felt very confused. 'I was sure she was going to be Gabriel's owner,' Mandy went on. 'She's got the same name.'

'Well, she's obviously not.' Susan tossed her head, causing her ponytail to bounce up and down. 'You heard what she said about hating horses. Huh! I'm certainly not going to be friends with *her* then!'

Mandy frowned. If Tania hated horses then why had she been drawing one on the cover of her notebook? Surely if you hated horses, you didn't spend your time drawing them? 'But . . .' she began.

'Shh!' said a teacher further down the corridor and Mandy quickly stopped talking.

Reaching the hall she sat down on the floor with the rest of her class. She could see Tania sitting in the row in front. The new girl was staring straight ahead, hugging her knees tightly against her chest.

Mr Wakeham, the head teacher, stood up on the platform and started to speak but Mandy hardly listened to a word. Tania's behaviour in the classroom had just been so strange.

She glanced across at the new girl just in time to see Tania look up at the ceiling. For a fleeting moment, a look of despair crossed Tania's face. She looked so utterly desolate that Mandy caught her breath in shock. She didn't think she had ever seen anyone look so unhappy. Tania dropped her eyes to the floor. When she looked up, Mandy saw that the emotion was gone and her face was blank once more.

After Assembly, Mandy's class trooped back to their classroom for English with Mr Meldrum. Mandy was very quiet. She couldn't stop thinking of the look she had seen on Tania's face. *What could have happened to make her look so miserable?* she thought.

Susan Collins was still angry at the way Tania had spoken to Mandy. 'I mean, who does she think she is?' she whispered to Mandy, as they walked down the corridor. 'You just don't go around blowing up at people like that.'

'Maybe she's unhappy about starting a new school,' Mandy said.

'Well, she still shouldn't have spoken to you like that,' said Susan. 'She's not going to make any friends that way.'

'It can't be easy for her, Susan,' Mandy protested, feeling a sudden urge to defend

Tania. 'Don't you remember what it was like when you started here?' Susan had moved from London to Welford and at first had found it hard to settle in. 'You weren't exactly easy to get on with.'

'I wasn't as bad as her!' Susan said indignantly. She stomped off rather huffily to her desk.

Mandy was determined to try again with Tania. When she sat down she turned round in her chair. 'I'm sorry if I upset you before,' she said with an apologetic smile. 'I didn't mean to.'

Tania tucked a strand of blonde hair behind her left ear and shrugged. 'It's OK,' she said. She looked away as if to end the conversation but Mandy wouldn't let her.

'Where was your last school?' she asked.

'York,' Tania replied shortly.

'How long were you there?' Mandy asked.

'Ages.'

'Was it good?'

'Yes.'

Mandy struggled to keep the conversation going. 'Why did you have to move?'

Tania's eyebrows drew together sharply. 'Why do *you* have to ask so many questions?' she snapped.

Mandy was shocked by her directness.
'Well . . . uh . . .'

'Look!' said Tania, glaring at her. 'I just want
to be left alone. OK?'

Mandy turned round in her seat, her cheeks
burning. Susan looked at her as if to say, 'I told
you so.' And for once, Mandy was actually glad
when Mr Meldrum walked into the classroom
and the lesson began.

At break Mandy met James and told him all
about the new girl. 'First of all she gets cross
with me because I ask her about Gabriel and
then she gets mad at me because I asked her
why she moved,' Mandy said, opening her
packet of crisps.

'She sounds odd,' said James, as they walked
over to sit on the wall.

Mandy nodded. 'I think she's unhappy.'

'I bet it can't be easy changing schools,' James
said. 'I wouldn't like it.'

Mandy was almost sure that there was
more to Tania's unhappiness than just moving
schools. She still had a clear memory of the
despair on Tania's face during that moment
in Assembly. What was it that was making her
so miserable?

'Isn't it strange her having the same name as the person Gabriel was supposed to have been delivered to?' James said. 'It's a real coincidence.'

Mandy nodded. James's words had made her think about Gabriel in the back garden at Animal Ark.

If Tania wasn't his owner, then who was?

Four

'Come on, James! I want to get home!' Mandy said, wheeling her bike quickly down the path. She was eager to get back to Animal Ark to discover if there was any news on Gabriel's owners.

As they reached the school gate they saw Tania getting into a rather battered-looking grey car. A woman with short blonde hair was sitting in the driver's seat.

'Bye, Tania,' Mandy called.

Tania didn't reply. She just got into the car and slammed the door. Since snapping at Mandy that morning she had hardly spoken to anyone all day.

'Friendly as ever!' muttered Susan Collins, who was walking past them and had witnessed the scene.

'Susan!' Mandy said, turning to her friend.

'What?' Susan demanded. 'I don't know why you keep sticking up for her, Mandy.'

'She's probably unhappy.'

'Huh!' was Susan's reply.

'I wonder where Tania lives,' Mandy said to James as they cycled off.

James wasn't listening; he was standing up on his pedals and accelerating up the hill. 'Race you when we get to the top!' he called over his shoulder.

Forgetting about Tania, Mandy accepted the challenge and charged after him.

A short while later, Mandy swerved up the Animal Ark driveway. Throwing her bike down outside the surgery she hurried into reception. What was the news about Gabriel?

Adam Hope was standing beside the reception desk, checking through the diary. 'Hello,' he said, looking up as she ran in. 'Had a good day at school?'

But Mandy only had one thing on her mind. 'Dad!' Her eyes searched his face. 'What's happened about Gabriel? Have you found his owners? Is he still here?'

'He's still here,' Mr Hope replied, closing the diary. 'But we *have* found his owners. The delivery company are supposed to be getting in touch with them.'

'So who does he belong to?' Mandy demanded.

'A family called the Bensters. They've just moved into the village. There was a mix-up with Gabriel and my exercise machine, like we thought. The delivery man was in a rush because he had just heard that his wife had gone into the hospital to have a baby. He didn't read the addresses properly and just assumed that the horse would be going to the vets.'

'So have the Bensters got your exercise machine then?' Mandy asked.

Mr Hope shook his head. 'The delivery man didn't have time to get to their house so he dropped it back at the depot. The company has promised to deliver it as soon as possible. They've also got Gabriel's passport there – something else the delivery man forgot. They're going to send it on to the Bensters.'

'So Gabriel's still here for the moment?' Mandy said, feeling pleased.

Mr Hope nodded. 'At least until the Bensters get in touch.'

'We had a new girl in school today called Tania Benster,' Mandy told him, dumping her bag on a chair.

Mr Hope looked surprised. 'Gabriel's owner?'

Mandy shook her head. 'She didn't know anything about him. It's really strange that she's got the same name though.' She shrugged off her coat. 'In fact, *she's* strange. She—'

Mandy broke off as the door opened and a woman with short blonde hair came in. She was wearing a baggy jumper and jeans. Her face was worried. 'Hello. I'm looking for Adam Hope,' she said.

Mr Hope stepped forward. 'That's me. What can I do for you?'

The woman smiled. 'My name's Sally Benster. I think you might have my daughter's Miniature horse here.'

'Ah, Gabriel's mystery owner! Yes, we've got him,' Mr Hope said. 'He's fine.'

Mrs Benster's whole face seemed to sag with relief. 'Oh, that's such good news.' She shook her head. 'I can't tell you how worried I've been. Thank you so much for looking after him.'

'No problem,' said Mr Hope. 'Meet my

daughter, Mandy. She's been doing all the hard work.'

'My friend James helped me,' Mandy put in. She smiled at the woman. 'We've loved looking after him. He's wonderful.'

Mrs Benster looked at Mandy's school uniform. 'You might have met my daughter. We've just moved here and she had her first day at school today. You're probably about the same age. She's twelve. She's called Tania.'

'Tania!' Mandy exclaimed, feeling confused. 'Yes, she was in my class.' She shook her head. 'But she *can't* be Gabriel's owner. She said she wasn't!'

'Oh.' Mandy saw Mrs Benster's face fall.

'Is there a problem?' Mr Hope asked.

Mrs Benster nodded. 'Yes.' She sighed. 'Gabriel *is* Tania's horse. He was a present for her birthday on Saturday. But . . . well, she doesn't want him.'

Mandy could hardly believe her ears. 'Doesn't want him! Why not?'

Mrs Benster ran a hand through her hair. 'It's a long story,' she said. 'I'm sure you're both busy and don't want to hear my problems. Having Gabriel must have inconvenienced you enough already.' She turned to Mr Hope. 'I'll arrange for him to be moved straight away.'

'There's no rush,' Mr Hope replied. 'Look, why don't you come and have a cup of tea? Surgery doesn't start tonight for another half hour. You can tell us the whole story. Maybe we can help.'

'Well . . .' Mrs Benster hesitated.

Mandy saw the indecision on her face. 'I'll put the kettle on,' she said heading for the door. She was dying to know what was going on. 'It's no trouble.'

Mrs Benster gave in. 'Thank you,' she said, smiling at her gratefully. 'That would be very nice.'

Once in the Animal Ark kitchen, Mrs Benster started to explain the situation. 'Tania's father and I got divorced recently,' she said, stirring sugar into her mug of tea. 'I moved to Welford to be near my family. My sister and niece live here – the Parker Smythes, do you know them?'

Mr Hope and Mandy nodded. *So Mrs Benster is Mrs Parker Smythe's sister*, Mandy thought. She wasn't what she had imagined at all!

'Tania chose to come and live with me,' Mrs Benster continued, 'which has meant that she's had to cope with quite a few changes. We've moved to a smaller house, got a smaller car, she's had to change schools and she's had to sell her pony.' She shook her head. 'Tania loved Star so much. It's hit her really hard.'

Mandy made the connection. 'So Star is Imogen's new pony?'

Mrs Benster nodded. 'It seemed like such a good idea. Sonia, my sister, was looking for a pony for Imogen. I thought that Tania would still be able to see Star, maybe even ride her occasionally.' She looked at her tea. 'But it hasn't worked out like that. At the moment, Tania's refusing to go anywhere near Star. She won't go and see her and she won't visit her father either. She just seems so unhappy.'

'So how does Gabriel fit into the picture?' Mr Hope asked curiously.

Sally Benster took a long sip of her drink. 'Well, Gabriel was Sonia's idea,' she explained. 'She had seen an article on Miniature horses in a magazine and thought that if Tania had a Miniature horse it would help make up for losing Star. It seemed an ideal solution. The garden at our new cottage is large enough for a Miniature horse and they're not too expensive to feed. I agreed and so Sonia bought Gabriel. He was going to be a surprise birthday present for Tania on Saturday. Anyway, then he didn't

arrive and so I had to tell Tania about him and
. . . well . . .' Her voice trailed off.

'She didn't react well?' Mr Hope asked quietly.

'It was dreadful,' said Mrs Benster, shaking
her head and looking upset. 'She just exploded,
said that she hated horses and that she never
wanted one again. She even threatened to run
away if I brought Gabriel to the cottage.' She
shook her head. 'I don't know what to do.'

Tania's strange behaviour that day at school
was suddenly starting to make sense to Mandy.
She tried to imagine what it must be like to lose
so many things at once: your home, your father,
your friends and your pony. *Poor Tania – and
poor Gabe*, she thought. 'What will happen to
Gabriel?' she asked Mrs Benster.

'Sonia has offered to let him stay in Star's
paddock up at Beacon House for the moment,'
Mrs Benster replied. 'We're just going to see
what happens. If Tania still feels the same way
after Christmas then I suppose I'll just have to
sell him on.'

Mandy felt her heart sink. She didn't want
Gabriel to move away having only just met him.

'I'm sure Tania'll come round,' Mr Hope said.

'I hope you're right,' sighed Mrs Benster. 'But
she can be so stubborn at times.' She put down

her mug. 'Thank you. To tell you the truth it's been a relief to talk about all this. You've been very kind.' She stood up. 'I'll arrange to have Gabriel moved as soon as possible.'

Mr Hope got to his feet. 'No need to do that. We can drop him off at Beacon House for you. His crate should fit into the Land-rover.' He walked to the back door. 'Now, why don't you come and meet him.'

Mrs Benster followed Mandy and Mr Hope through to the back garden. 'Oh, he's tiny!' she cried as she saw Gabe grazing happily, wearing his New Zealand rug. She went over to stroke him. 'Isn't he adorable?'

Yes, thought Mandy as the little spotted horse looked up at them with pricked ears, *he is*. But the challenge was to make Tania realise that too.

The following morning, just as it was getting light, Mr Hope stopped the Land-rover outside Beacon House. 'I'll go and let Mrs Parker Smythe know we're here.' He jumped out and crunched across the gravel to the grand front door.

Mandy looked at the large white house. It was flanked on one side by a tennis court, on the other by a helicopter pad. 'Imagine living in a house like this,' she said to James. 'Just think how many animals you could have!'

James yawned and nodded half-heartedly. Mandy grinned. James hated getting up early but he had been determined to come with them to drop Gabriel off.

Mr Hope hurried back. 'We're going to drive Gabriel round to the stables and unload him there,' he said.

The gardens at the back of Beacon House were beautifully landscaped with a pond and an orchard and rows and rows of carefully tended flower-beds. The stables were a little to one side behind a high privet hedge. 'I never even knew there were stables here,' Mandy said to her dad as he drove down a small driveway and stopped outside a red-brick block of three stables and a tack room. Behind the stables was a paddock.

'That must be Star!' Mandy exclaimed, seeing a pretty palomino pony grazing. Almost before Mr Hope had stopped the Land-rover, Mandy was leaping out. She raced over to the paddock. James followed her.

'Isn't she lovely?' Mandy breathed as they leaned over the five-bar gate and looked at the pony. Star lifted her head and regarded them from a distance. Her coat was the colour of pale gold and her mane and tail were cream. On her forehead was a diamond-shaped splash.

'That's Star,' said a high-pitched voice behind them. They turned and saw a mousy-haired, slightly overweight girl coming towards them. 'She's my new pony.'

'Hi, Imogen,' Mandy with a smile. When she had first met Imogen, the little girl had been spoilt and rude but ever since she had been given the rabbits – Button and Barney – she had become far less selfish and more friendly and outgoing.

Imogen reached into the pocket of her bright red anorak and took out a carrot. 'Star!' she called. 'Come and say hello.' Star walked over to the gate but stopped just out of reach. Imogen held out the carrot temptingly. 'Come on!' The palomino pony came forward but as soon as Imogen tried to take hold of her headcollar she jumped back and trotted away.

Mandy saw Imogen's face fall. 'Does she do that often?' she asked the little girl.

Imogen nodded. 'It took two of the gardeners half an hour to catch her yesterday.' Mandy saw her lower lip quiver slightly. 'I don't think she

likes me.' Imogen stared at her pony who was now grazing again.

'Oh, I'm sure she does,' Mandy said quickly.

'Ponies are often difficult to catch,' James added. 'It doesn't mean they don't like you.'

'Really?' said Imogen, looking hopeful.

Just then, Mr Hope called to them. 'Mandy! James! Can you give me a hand getting Gabriel out, please?' He had opened the back of the Land-rover. Beside him stood a lady who was looking rather uncertainly at the large crate. She was wearing a very new-looking green waxed jacket, a yellow silk scarf, leather gloves and a pair of light beige trousers that had been tucked into the cleanest green wellies that Mandy had ever seen.

'Hello, Mrs Parker Smythe,' Mandy said, reaching the Land-rover.

Mrs Parker Smythe smiled. 'Good morning, Mandy.' Even though it was early in the morning, Mandy noticed that she was already perfectly made-up. 'Has Immi been showing you her new pony?'

Mandy nodded.

Mr Hope attached a ramp to the back of the Land-rover and opened Gabriel's crate. Gabriel looked out and surveyed the scene. What have we here? he seemed to say.

'It's all right, Gabe,' Mandy murmured, taking him by the headcollar. 'This is where you're going to live for a while.' She led him down the ramp and let him have a good look round.

Imogen fed him carrots from her pocket, laughing as his lips tickled her hand. 'He's cute!'

'He looks even smaller here than he did at his breeders,' Mrs Parker Smythe said, patting him rather gingerly.

'I wonder how he'll get on with Star,' James said.

'There's only one way to find out,' Mr Hope replied.

Mandy led Gabriel to the paddock. Seeing Star, his ears pricked up and he quickened his pace. Star walked curiously towards the gate. 'Should I just let him go, Dad?' Mandy asked.

Mr Hope nodded as he unlatched the gate. 'They should be fine.'

Mandy unclipped the leadrope and Gabriel trotted eagerly into the field towards Star. He stopped a short distance away. Both ponies extended their heads until their muzzles were almost touching. There was a long pause while they blew down their nostrils at each other. Mandy crossed her fingers. She had seen ponies do this before and knew that sometimes they would squeal and strike out at each other, but this time it didn't happen. Star and Gabriel dropped their heads and started to graze contentedly side by side.

'They're friends!' said Imogen and everyone smiled.

Mr Hope turned to Mrs Parker Smythe. 'Will you be all right looking after them both?'

'I hope so,' Mrs Parker Smythe replied, a slight frown creasing her face. 'Sally assured me that Gabriel shouldn't be too much trouble but you see, Imogen's father and I don't really know that much about horses. We've got a part-time groom starting after Christmas. I thought we'd be all right until then because Tania was supposed to have been helping out, but . . . well . . .' She cast a quick look at Imogen. 'That hasn't worked out.'

'Tania's too busy moving house at the moment,' Imogen announced. 'That's why she can't have Gabriel and why she can't help, isn't it, Mummy?'

'That's right, darling,' Mrs Parker Smythe said.

Mandy and James exchanged glances. Obviously Imogen had not been told the real story.

Mrs Parker Smythe looked at the ponies and sighed. 'I suppose Immi and I will just have to manage as best we can until the groom starts.'

Mandy suddenly had an idea. 'We could help,' she offered eagerly. 'Couldn't we, James? We break up from school on Friday.'

'We'd love to,' James said.

'Oh yes, Mummy! Yes!' said Imogen. 'It would be fun!'

Mandy looked hopefully at Mrs Parker

Smythe. 'Are you sure?' Mrs Parker Smythe said to her.

'Definitely!'

Mrs Parker Smythe turned to Mr Hope. 'Would that be all right with you, Mr Hope?'

'Certainly,' said Mr Hope. 'It seems an ideal solution. Good for the horses, good for you . . .'

'And great for us!' said Mandy, grinning at James. Now, they wouldn't have to say goodbye to Gabriel after all. They could come and see him everyday.

Gabriel wandered near the gate. Imogen ducked underneath the fence and took a handful of carrots over to him.

Mrs Parker Smythe shook her head as she watched Gabriel gently take the carrots from Imogen's outstretched palm. 'Sometimes I wonder if I've done the right thing,' she said quietly so Imogen wouldn't hear. 'Buying Gabriel seemed like such a good idea at the time. I thought Tania would be delighted. The woman at the breeders told me that Miniature horses have a nickname – they are called the Ambassadors of Goodwill. I suppose I hoped that Gabriel could be an Ambassador of Goodwill for Tania, helping her get used to the changes in her life, but, well,' she shook her head, 'I'm beginning to wonder whether I've done more harm than good.' She sighed and then seemed to pull herself together. 'Can I offer you a cup of coffee or tea, Mr Hope?' she said.

Mr Hope shook his head. 'We'd better get on or Mandy and James will be late for school.' He started walking towards the Land-rover with James. 'Come on, Mandy,' he called over his shoulder.

Mandy was looking at Gabriel. Tania just *had* to accept him.

'Mandy!' her father called.

'Coming!' Mandy called. She looked again at the little horse. 'I'll persuade her, Gabe,' she whispered. 'Just you wait and see.'

Five

When she got to school, Mandy hurried to her class's cloakroom. She stopped in the doorway. Tania was taking off her coat, her back to the door. Mandy was suddenly aware of how awkward a meeting this could be. What did she say? Did she admit to knowing that Gabriel was Tania's or did she pretend she didn't know anything?

Tania turned and froze, a look of confusion and embarrassment crossing her face as she saw Mandy standing there.

Mandy made a quick decision. It was better to be upfront. 'Hi,' she said, going forward with a friendly smile. 'I met your mum last night and she told me that Gabriel was yours. She told me about you not wanting him and . . .' she hesitated, '. . . and about the divorce.'

Tania flinched, two bright red spots of colour springing into her cheeks.

Mandy hurried on. 'My dad and I took him up to your aunt's this morning. We put him in Star's field. She seems to like him.'

'I don't care,' Tania said in a low, determined voice. She went to walk past Mandy. 'I told Mum to get rid of him.'

'But why?' Mandy said, stopping her. 'He's lovely.'

'He's a Miniature horse!' Tania exclaimed, shaking her arm free from Mandy. 'What good are they?'

'Lots!' Mandy said. 'They pull traps, you can train them to be driven, and there are shows for them. They can even be ridden by small children.' She had been reading her father's book.

'Exactly!' Tania said angrily. 'They're for babies! They're not proper horses. They're just for people who can't afford proper horses.'

'That's not true!' Mandy said. 'Look, just come and see him. You'll adore him.'

Tania shook her head. 'No way! Mum should

never have taken him to Auntie Sonia's. I told her I didn't want him. Well, I'm not going to change my mind.' She pushed past Mandy.

'But he'd make you so happy!' Mandy exclaimed after her.

Tania swung round. 'Happy?' There was a pause during which she looked at Mandy in utter disbelief and then she shook her head. 'How can I ever be happy again?' She ran out of the cloakroom, but not before Mandy had seen tears welling up in her eyes.

At break Mandy talked things over with James. 'I know it's just because she's angry and upset about the divorce and everything,' she sighed as they sat on the wall outside. 'But if she actually came to see Gabriel, I'm sure she'd want to keep him. The trouble is how do we *get* her to meet him? She refused to come and see him.'

James looked thoughtful. 'It's almost the holidays. Maybe we could take Gabriel for walks down to her house and hope to bump into her.'

'Of course!' Mandy exclaimed. 'If Tania won't come to see Gabe then we'll take him to see her! That's a brilliant idea, James!'

'We could take him on Saturday,' said James.

'And then again on Sunday.'

'And then on Monday.' Mandy said. 'If she sees him often enough she's bound to fall in love with him!' She grinned. 'It's a great plan! We'll have changed her mind by Christmas, you'll see!'

But when she told her mum that evening, Mrs Hope looked doubtful. 'Remember, Tania's been through a very difficult time, Mandy,' she warned, as she put a young rabbit with a freshly bandaged leg back into a cage. 'It may take some time before she's ready to come to terms with her new life.'

Mandy helped clear up the old dressing. 'But if she keeps seeing Gabriel surely she won't be able to resist him.'

Mrs Hope tucked a strand of hair behind her ear. 'It's worth a try, but don't be disappointed if it doesn't work, love. I think it sounds like Tania needs some time and space at the moment.'

Mandy understood what her mum was saying but it didn't matter. She still felt convinced that the plan would work.

Mrs Hope opened the door of Honey's cage. The golden retriever was looking far more cheerful than she had a few days ago.

'She's much better,' Mandy said, as Honey came out, wagging her tail.

Mrs Hope nodded. 'I rang her owners. They're coming to collect her tomorrow.' She opened the cage door and bent down to inspect Honey's stitches. 'Healing up nicely,' she said.

'I'll miss you,' Mandy said, kneeling down and stroking Honey's face. 'But at least you'll be home for Christmas.' Honey wagged her tail. Mandy smiled. It was always hard saying goodbye to animals, but there was nothing better than seeing an animal being reunited with its happy owners. Mandy gently scratched Honey's silky ears. Much as she would miss her, she knew that Honey would be glad to go home.

The next morning, before school, Mandy cycled up to Beacon House to check on Gabriel and Star. She tapped the security code which Mrs Parker Smythe had given her the day before into the black box by the entrance. The electric gates swung open smoothly. Mandy cycled up the long drive and round to the stables.

'Hi!' Imogen came running to meet her. 'Will you help me catch Star?'

They walked down to the paddock and called

the ponies. Gabriel walked eagerly towards
them but Star tossed her head and walked away.
'She did this yesterday,' Imogen told Mandy.
'I couldn't catch her at all and there was no
one to help. Daddy was at work and Mummy
had friends for lunch and it was the gardeners'
day off.'

'Don't worry, we'll get her,' Mandy said. She
looked at Star, who had stopped a little way
down the field. 'If we take Gabriel in and then
bring out a bucket with some pony-nuts in she
might come.'

Imogen nodded. 'OK. But I bet it takes
ages.' She opened the gate for Mandy to lead
Gabriel through.

'Come on, Gabe,' Mandy said, clicking
her tongue.

Gabriel looked round at Star and whickered
gently.

'Look!' said Imogen suddenly.

Star had started walking towards them; she
was looking at Gabriel. Imogen held out a carrot
and Star walked all the way over. The pony
stopped and glanced at Gabriel, who gave
another reassuring whicker and then Star took
the carrot daintily from her hand.

'Good girl! Imogen cried, clipping on the

leadrope. She turned to Mandy, her eyes shining with excitement. 'She's never done that before!'

Mandy grinned. 'It must be Gabe. He's a good influence!'

They took the two ponies to the stables and fed them their breakfasts. Then Mandy showed Imogen how to check them over for any cuts or lumps.

'I know how to groom,' Imogen said, taking a dandy-brush out of her grooming kit box. 'We learnt at my riding school.'

The two girls settled down to grooming the ponies. Imogen soon had a smudge on her nose and dust in her hair. Mandy smiled. It was amazing how animals brought out the best in people, she thought, as she watched Imogen kiss Star's nose.

'Mummy says I can't ride her till the weekend when you and James are here,' Imogen said. 'But I'm going to groom her lots.' She smiled happily and picked up a soft body brush to use on Star's face. 'Star's won lots of prizes. Tania used to have all her rosettes on a wall in her bedroom. Mummy says that when Tania's not as busy she's going to come and teach me. I can't wait.'

Imogen chattered on until it was time for

Mandy to change into her school clothes and cycle back down the hill. 'See you tomorrow,' she called to Imogen as she got on her bike. Imogen was still grooming Star. She waved happily and Mandy cycled away.

For the rest of the week, Tania ignored Mandy at school. She hardly spoke to anyone but sat by herself at lunch and break-time, seeming to retreat more and more into her own unhappy thoughts. Mandy became more and more convinced that Tania needed Gabriel. Surely, she wouldn't be able to stay so miserable if she had a horse to think about and love.

It was raining with a fine drizzle when Mandy got up on Saturday morning but she didn't care. It was the first day of the holidays and she leaped out of bed with a broad grin on her face.

'You look happy!' Mrs Hope said, as Mandy raced down the stairs.

'That's because I am!' Mandy exclaimed. 'Two weeks without school and it's almost Christmas! Only one more week to go. I can't wait!'

Mrs Hope laughed. 'Do you want a lift up to Beacon House later?'

'Yes, please!' Mandy said eagerly. 'I'll ring James and tell him to come round.' She helped herself to a satsuma. Today was the first day of their plan to get Tania to accept Gabriel. She was determined that it was going to work!

When Mrs Hope dropped Mandy and James at Beacon House after morning surgery, Imogen came running out to meet them. 'Hooray!' she said. 'I can ride Star now!'

James looked at Mandy. 'We'll walk Gabe later,' she said. She could see from Imogen's face that the little girl was about to burst with excitement.

Star shook her head and stamped her feet as they tacked her up and Imogen mounted. 'She looks a bit lively,' James whispered to Mandy as Imogen set off around the paddock.

'Are you all right?' Mandy called to Imogen. Star was pulling and tossing her head.

'Fine!' Imogen called back but Mandy could hear a shake in her voice. Then Star shied and Imogen shortened her reins, making Star pull even more. Imogen leaned forward rather nervously. Star sidestepped and jogged. *She doesn't look fine*, Mandy thought.

'What shall we do?' James said.

Mandy had a sudden idea. 'Back in a minute,' she said, setting off for the stables. She returned a few minutes later leading Gabriel.

'What are you doing?' Imogen called.

'He was lonely,' Mandy lied. Gabriel looked at Star for a few moments and then put his head down to graze. Just as Mandy had hoped, having Gabriel nearby seemed to relax the palomino pony. She stopped jogging as much and Imogen loosened the reins.

Mandy hugged Gabe. The effect he had on Star was wonderful. Mandy crossed her fingers. She hoped he would have the same effect on Tania too!

After brushing Star down, Imogen went off Christmas shopping with her mum and dad and Mandy and James were at last free to take Gabriel down to the village.

It was quiet on the road. Only the soft clip-clopping of Gabe's unshod hooves and the occasional cry of a bird circling overhead broke the stillness of the air.

James frowned. 'What if Tania isn't in?'

'We keep coming back until she is,' Mandy replied. She was determined their plan was going to work.

They approached Willow Cottage. 'What should we do when we get there?' James asked, pushing his hair back from his forehead. 'Just walk him up and down outside?'

Mandy nodded. She hadn't really thought beyond the initial plan of taking him to Tania's house. A thought struck her. What if Tania just stayed inside and refused to come out and see Gabriel? Knowing Tania, it seemed quite likely. Mandy pushed the thought away. *Think positive*, she told herself firmly.

'It doesn't look like there's anyone in.' James said as they reached the cottage. There were no lights on inside.

'Tania might be there,' Mandy said. 'Come on, let's walk him around.' They led Gabriel up and down the road several times. But there wasn't a sign of movement from the house. At last even Mandy had to admit that they were wasting their time.

'So what do we do now?' James asked, stopping.

'Come back later,' Mandy said, trying to sound positive.

James raised his eyebrows slightly. 'So we walk all the way back to Beacon House and then turn round and come back?'

'Yes,' Mandy replied, beginning to realise the second problem with their plan. It was all very well to say they would keep coming back until Tania was in but it was actually quite a walk from Beacon House down to Willow Cottage. She had an idea. 'We could take him to visit Susan and then come and see if Tania is in on our way back.'

Susan lived outside the village, further down the Walton Road. James shrugged. 'OK. It's better than walking all the way back up the hill straight away, I suppose.'

They set off down the road. 'There's Prince!' said Mandy, pointing. The bay gelding was grazing in a field just to the side of The Beeches, Susan's large house. A figure was standing beside the stone wall watching him.

'Isn't that Tania?' James said.

Mandy nodded. 'This is perfect! Now she's going to have to see Gabe!'

As they drew closer, Tania heard them. She started to walk swiftly away in the opposite direction.

'Tania!' Mandy called. 'Wait!'

Tania stopped and turned slowly round.

Gabriel, eager to say hello to this new person dragged Mandy forward until he reached Tania. Hello, he seemed to say, nudging her with his nose. Who are you? Have you got any treats? For a fleeting second a smile lit up Tania's face as she looked down at him and automatically she reached out to stroke his neck.

'He's lovely isn't he?' Mandy said eagerly.

Tania pulled her hand away and stepped back. Gabriel followed her. She pushed him away. Gabriel pushed back. A new game! he seemed to think. He pulled determinedly towards Tania with Mandy hanging on at the end of the leadrope. No matter how far Tania retreated he followed her. Despite herself, Tania's lips started to twitch. 'Go away!' she half laughed, pushing him again. 'Go on!'

Gabe refused to listen. Mandy was delighted.

'He likes you,' she said to Tania. 'Look at the way he is trying to get to you.'

The smile instantly vanished from the other girl's face. 'I don't want him to like me!' she said.

Mandy looked at her in astonishment. 'Why not?'

Tania's eyes looked almost desperate. 'I just don't! OK?'

'But, Tania . . .'

Tania turned and ran down the road.

James looked at Mandy in confusion. 'What did she mean by that?'

'I don't know,' said Mandy, equally mystified. She frowned after the disappearing figure. What possible reason could Tania have for not wanting Gabriel to like her? It just didn't make any sense. She patted the Miniature horse's neck. 'Well, *we* like you, anyway,' she told him.

'So what are we going to do now?' James asked.

'Try again tomorrow,' Mandy said. Determination flooded through her. 'Whatever she says, we're not going to give up!'

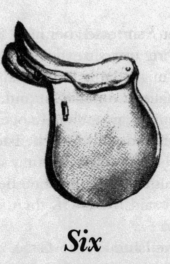

Six

'Mummy says I can take Star a little way down the road today if you come with me,' Imogen said, as she ran to meet Mandy and James the next morning.

Star tossed her head as they tacked her up. She stamped her foot and sidestepped as Mandy tried to tighten up the girth. It was windy and the wind seemed to be making her livelier than ever.

'Steady, girl,' said James, who was holding on to her bridle.

Mandy tried again but Star danced about. 'I'll do it up the last few holes just before you get on,' she said to Imogen, who was putting on her hard hat. Star tossed her head high. Mandy frowned. 'Are you sure this is a good idea, Imogen? It might be better to wait until a less windy day before you take her out.'

'No, I want to go today,' Imogen said, with just a hint of the spoilt child she had once been creeping into her voice. 'Mummy said I could.'

Mandy reluctantly gave way. If Mrs Parker Smythe had said it was OK then she couldn't really argue.

'Maybe we should get Gabe,' James said to her in a low voice. 'It might keep Star a bit calmer.'

'Good idea,' Mandy said, taking the reins from him.

'I want to get on!' said Imogen.

'Let me tighten her girth first,' Mandy said, as James set off for the paddock to catch Gabriel. She lifted the saddle flap, trying to hold on to the reins at the same time. There was a gust of wind. Star suddenly whipped round, Mandy lost hold of the reins and the next instant Star was cantering off down the drive.

'Star!' cried Imogen in panic.

'Oh no!' gasped Mandy.

'Quick!' said James. Mandy and James dashed after the fast disappearing pony.

'It'll be OK!' James said, as they charged along the drive. 'The gates will be shut at the bottom. They always are. We'll catch her there.'

'When we get near her don't run!' said Mandy.

They raced round the bend in the drive expecting to see Star waiting by the gates. But the gates were wide open. Star was nowhere to be seen.

'Come on!' James exclaimed to Mandy. 'We've got to stop her!' They started running down the hill.

Mandy's heart pounded. Although the twisty, narrow road that led down from Beacon House to the village was quiet, the road at the bottom of the hill could be very busy. If Star got on to it, there was no knowing what could happen. Mandy knew she would never forgive herself if anything happened to Star. *Oh why didn't I keep hold of the reins?* she thought.

'There!' gasped James as they ran round a bend in the road. They both stopped dead. Star was grazing in a gateway, just ahead.

Mandy's heart leaped. 'Star!' she called. She rustled a sweet paper in her pocket and the pony looked up. Mandy knew that they had to keep as calm as possible. What they didn't want was Star to take fright and canter off again.

'There's a good girl!' Mandy said in as soothing a voice as she could. She walked slowly forward, rustling the sweet paper again and holding out her hand. 'Come here. Good girl.'

Pricking her ears curiously, Star took a step towards her but then, just at the wrong moment, Imogen came running round the bend. 'Star!' she cried out in delight. The pony started in alarm and, wheeling round, trotted off down the road, the reins flapping dangerously near her legs.

'Imogen!' Mandy exclaimed in dismay.

A figure came walking round a bend in the road ahead.

'It's Tania!' cried James.

Tania saw Star trotting towards her and leaped into the pony's path. 'Star!' she cried. The pony stopped dead and snorted wildly. Tania held out a hand. 'Here, girl,' she said softly.

Grabbing on to Imogen in case she made any sudden move, Mandy and James watched as Star lowered her head and walked straight over to Tania and pushed affectionately at her with her head. Tania gently touched Star's face.

Imogen pulled free from Mandy and James and raced down the road. 'Tania! Tania!' she cried, her voice high and excited. 'You caught her! Thank you! Thank you so much!'

Star leaped back and Tania grabbed her reins only just in time. 'Stop it!' she called out to Imogen. 'Stop running!'

The little girl stopped. The shock on Tania's face turned to anger. She marched towards Imogen. 'Haven't you any sense, Imogen?' she demanded, her eyes blazing. 'What do you think you are doing, running towards a pony who's excited?' She didn't give Imogen a chance to speak. 'And what's Star doing loose on the road anyway?'

'She escaped,' Imogen stammered, taken aback by Tania's anger. 'I was about to get on.'

'She could have ended up in an accident!' Tania exclaimed.

'I know . . . I'm sorry,' Imogen whispered, her face starting to crumple.

'Sorry isn't enough!' Tania's voice was shaking with emotion. 'What good is it to be sorry when Star's lying dead at the bottom of the road? You don't deserve to have a pony, Imogen!'

Mandy hurried up. 'Tania!' she exclaimed. 'It's not Imogen's fault.' Tania glared at her. 'It's not,' Mandy insisted. '*I* was holding Star when she escaped. If anyone's to blame, it's me, not Imogen.'

Tania paused. She glanced at Star and suddenly the anger seemed to drain from her face. She thrust the reins at Mandy. 'Here,' she said. 'Take her.' Before Mandy could say anything she had turned and walked off down the road.

'Tania!' Imogen called after her, the tears rolling down her cheeks.

Mandy hesitated. Should she go after Tania? Or should she stay and comfort Imogen?

James seemed to read her thoughts. 'Go on,' he said quietly, reaching for Star's reins. 'I'll look after Imogen.' He put an arm round Imogen's shoulders. 'Come on, Immi. Let's take Star back.'

Mandy set off after Tania. She had stopped a little way down the road and was staring down the hill, her back to Mandy.

Mandy slowed as she reached her. *This could be difficult*, she thought. 'Are you all right?' she asked.

Tania nodded and sniffed but didn't look round.

'I know Imogen shouldn't have run up like that, Tania,' Mandy said. 'But it wasn't her fault that Star escaped.' There was a pause and then she saw Tania give a faint nod. 'Star's really too much for her,' said Mandy, feeling encouraged. 'Couldn't you come and help?'

There was no reply.

'Tania?'

Tania swung round. Her pale cheeks were damp with tears. 'You don't get it, do you?' she cried intensely, a catch in her voice. 'Star should be *mine*, not Imogen's. Every time I see her it reminds me of—' She broke off, shaking her head. 'It just reminds me,' she said more quietly.

'But you've got Gabriel now,' Mandy said.

'Gabriel?' said Tania. 'A useless Miniature horse!'

Anger rose in Mandy. 'He's not useless!' she exclaimed. 'He's friendly and cheeky and affectionate and he'd love you if you gave him a chance.'

'No,' Tania said fiercely, half turning away.

'Why not?' Mandy demanded. 'He's . . .'

'Don't you see?' Tania cried, spinning round passionately. 'If you love something you only lose it!' Her eyes searched Mandy's astonished face. 'If you love nothing then you've got nothing to lose and nothing can hurt you ever again!' Her shoulders suddenly sagged. 'Oh, what's the use?' she said bitterly. 'What would

you understand, anyway?' Turning abruptly she
ran down the hill.

Mandy stared after her, feeling shocked. *Poor
Tania*, she thought. *Imagine feeling like that.* She
wondered what to do and had to admit that she
didn't know the answer. Tania's feelings were a
lot more complicated than she'd thought.
Feeling uncomfortable, she turned and walked
up the road towards Beacon House.

Mandy was quiet for the rest of the day. When
she got home she worked hard in the surgery,
trying to push the incident that afternoon to
the back of her mind.

After the last patient had gone, Mr Hope
came over to her. 'So, do you want to see my
new exercise machine then?'

'Has it arrived?' Mandy asked. All week
they had been waiting for redelivery of Mr
Hope's parcel.

'It certainly has. Come and see.'

Mandy followed him through to the house
and into the lounge. The air smelled of pine
from the Christmas tree in the corner. 'It's all
in bits,' she said, looking at the pieces of metal
scattered on the lounge floor.

Mr Hope nodded. 'There are instructions

that tell you how to put it together.'

'But you're not going to start now,' Mrs Hope said, popping her head round the door. 'Supper's almost ready.'

'I'll just go and wash my hands,' said Mr Hope.

Mandy picked up the plan. On one side it had a picture of the assembled machine with a tanned, muscular man in yellow Lycra shorts working out on it. 'Do you think Dad will end up like that?' she grinned, showing the picture to her mum as they went through to the kitchen together.

Mrs Hope laughed. 'I doubt it.' She took a closer look. 'In fact, I hope not!'

After supper, Mandy and Mr Hope attempted to put the machine together. 'Now where does this piece fit?' he said, holding up an aluminium tube.

'I don't know,' Mandy replied. She looked at the plan and then at the half-constructed exercise machine in front of them. 'We've got it wrong. We're going to have to start again.'

Mrs Hope was sitting on the sofa, watching them, her legs curled underneath her. 'I thought that the leaflet says that this machine can be put together in five easy steps.'

Mandy and Mr Hope just looked at her. 'These instructions just don't seem to make sense,' Mandy said, turning the piece of paper round and looking at it from different angles. The phone rang and Mr Hope, who was on call that night, got up to answer it.

'Here, let me see,' Mrs Hope said to Mandy. She reached for the piece of paper and examined it thoughtfully. 'Shouldn't you have attached that bit first?' she said, pointing to a piece of equipment. 'Look.' She got up from the sofa. 'This is piece A.'

Mr Hope popped his head round the door. 'I've got to go to Drysdale Farm. They've got a horse down with colic.' He glanced at the machine and coughed. 'I'll er . . . finish that when I get back.'

As he left the room, Mrs Hope turned to Mandy. 'This doesn't look too difficult,' she said, kneeling down beside her. 'Now A is going to connect to B like this. You've just got to be logical. Pass me that piece over there. Come on, we can do this.'

Mandy and Mrs Hope started assembling the machine. 'So how were the horses today?' Mrs Hope asked as they worked.

Somewhat shame-faced, Mandy told her

about Star escaping. 'I should never have let go of the reins,' she said. 'But it all happened so quickly. Before I knew what was happening she was cantering off down the drive.'

'At least she's all right,' Mrs Hope said comfortingly.

'Thanks to Tania,' said Mandy. 'If she hadn't been walking up the road then . . .' Her voice trailed off – she didn't like to think what might have happened if Tania hadn't been there to stop Star.

'How is Tania? Is your plan with Gabriel working?'

'Not very well,' Mandy sighed.

Mrs Hope looked sympathetic. 'I told you not to expect miracles. But maybe in a little while she'll come round.'

Or maybe not, thought Mandy. She could still hear Tania's words from that afternoon. If you love something you only lose it, she had said. If she felt like that then she was never going to let herself love Gabriel.

'Mandy?' Mrs Hope said, looking keenly at her. 'Is something the matter?'

Normally Mandy told her mum everything, but now she shook her head. 'No, nothing,' she said quickly. She didn't want to talk about that afternoon. She was sure that Tania wouldn't want her words repeated.

'Are you sure?' Mrs Hope persisted. 'You were very quiet when you got back this afternoon.'

'I'm sure!' Mandy met her mother's steady gaze. 'Well, I *am* worried about Imogen,' she said. It was really only a half-lie. She *was* feeling anxious about her and her new pony. 'Star's a real handful. When we got back today Imogen rode her in the paddock, but she's very lively.'

Mrs Hope appeared to accept the explanation. 'Star's probably unsettled by the move and the change of rider,' she said. 'She's used to being ridden by an experienced twelve-year-old, and now she's suddenly got an inexperienced seven-year-old on her back and is deciding to play up and see what she can get away with. Ponies can be naughty like that. I think you'll find she settles down in time.'

I hope so, thought Mandy. It was obvious how much Imogen loved her new pony, and it would be dreadful if Star proved too much for her to handle.

Mrs Hope sat back and looked at the fully-assembled exercise machine. 'There,' she said, satisfied. 'The instructions *were* correct. Five

easy steps and it's assembled.' Her eyes teased
Mandy. 'Now why couldn't you and your father
do that?'

Seven

As Mandy and James cycled up to Beacon House the next morning, Mandy told him about her mum putting the exercise machine together. 'You should have seen Dad's face when he came in,' she grinned. 'He couldn't stop staring.'

'Has he tried it out yet?' James said.

Mandy nodded. 'He was going to do fifteen minutes before breakfast,' she said.

'And?'

'He managed five!'

James grinned. 'Maybe he'll build up gradually.'

'Hmm,' Mandy said, not convinced. 'I think it was harder work than he was expecting.' They cycled on a bit.

'Shall we take Gabriel to Tania's this morning?' James asked.

'No.' Mandy saw James look at her in surprise. 'I . . . I don't think it's a good idea to take him there every day,' she said, blushing slightly.

'Why not?' James said, astonished. 'I thought that was the plan.'

'I know but . . . well, she was a bit upset yesterday.'

To her relief James didn't ask any other questions, just shrugged. 'OK.'

'We could take him out for a little walk down the drive though,' Mandy suggested. 'It would do him good to have some exercise.'

Imogen was out visiting a friend that morning so Mandy and James caught Gabriel and walked him down the driveway. As they left they could hear Star whinnying to him. He turned round and called back to her.

'I'm glad they're such good friends,' Mandy said. They reached the road and let him graze on the grass at the side.

Mandy looked over the stone wall. From here, she could see the road as it wound its way down the hillside. She stiffened. Sitting on a wall, a bit further down the road was Tania. Mandy was about to draw back when Tania looked up and saw her. Feeling almost as if she had been spying, Mandy half raised her hand in an embarrassed wave. She moved back from the wall. She guessed Tania wanted to be alone.

But to her surprise, a few minutes later, Tania came walking round the corner towards them.

'It's Tania!' James said to Mandy. 'Hi!' he called out.

Tania reached them. 'Hi.' Her cheeks were slightly flushed and she spoke quickly as if she had something that she wanted to get out. 'Look, I'm . . . um . . . sorry about yesterday,' she said, looking at Mandy. 'I shouldn't have shouted at Imogen – or you.'

Mandy felt very awkward. 'That's all right,' she muttered. 'Forget it.'

There was a silence. It seemed to go on for ever. 'Well . . . um . . . I better go,' Tania said. 'I guess that's all I came to say.' Her shoulders sagged and she turned.

An impulse seized Mandy. 'Tania!' she called. 'We were just going to take Gabe for a walk. Why don't you come with us?' Tania hesitated. 'Come on.'

'OK,' Tania said with a shy smile. 'Thanks.'

They started up the road with James leading Gabriel. The little horse walked eagerly, his ears pricked. He seemed to love exploring new places.

'Where does this road lead to?' Tania asked, after a bit.

'Up to the Beacon. There's a Celtic cross. You should be able to see it soon,' Mandy replied.

They passed some high yew hedges. 'That's Upper Welford Hall,' James told Tania. 'Sam Western lives there. He's a big dairy farmer.'

'Not a very nice one,' said Mandy. She and James exchanged glances. They had experienced several unpleasant run-ins with Sam Western in the past.

'What about up there?' Tania asked, pointing up an unmade track.

'That's High Cross Farm,' Mandy said. 'Lydia Fawcett owns it. She keeps goats.'

'And that's Piper's Wood,' said James, pointing to a wood that bordered on to Sam Western's land.

Gabriel pulled James over to a patch of grass and they stopped to let him graze. From their viewpoint they could see right the way down the valley. The village of Welford nestled at the bottom. Mandy spotted the church, the Fox and Goose and Animal Ark. 'There's your house,' she pointed out to Tania.

Tania started for a long moment and then suddenly shook her head. 'I'm never going to get used to living here,' she said, half to herself.

Mandy looked at Tania's unhappy face. 'You will,' she said. 'Susan Collins moved here from London and she got used to it.'

'But I don't *want* to get used to it!' Tania's voice grew passionate. 'I hate it! I want to be in my old house with our swimming-pool and stables. I want to be near my friends. I don't want to be here!' Tears welled up in her eyes. As if sensing her unhappiness, Gabriel stepped closer to her. Almost without thinking, Tania put a hand on his neck. 'It's horrible not knowing anyone,' she said. 'I speak to my friends on the phone but it's not the same.' She swallowed. 'Nothing's the same.'

'Do you see your dad much?' James asked.

Tania's face darkened. 'Never. I hate him. He's ruined my life.' She dashed a tear from her cheek and turned abruptly. 'I'd better go,' she said.

'We'll come with you,' Mandy said. 'It's probably been a long enough walk for Gabe.'

They started walking back down the road. *Poor Tania*, Mandy thought, glancing across. *It can't be easy for her. She must be so lonely not having any friends here.* An idea formed in her mind.

'James and I are going Christmas shopping tomorrow morning,' she said to Tania as they reached the Parker Smythes' house. 'We're meeting at nine-thirty. Would you like to come?'

Tania looked surprised. 'You wouldn't mind?' she said, looking from Mandy to James.

'Of course not,' James said.

Mandy grinned at her. 'You'll have to put up with helping me choose socks for my grandad, though.'

Tania almost smiled. 'I guess I can cope.' She looked Mandy straight in the eye. 'Thanks,' she said.

'We'll call for you!' Mandy called as Tania set off down the hill. 'Nine-thirty, remember!'

'See you then!' Tania called back and Mandy noticed that her step seemed springier than before.

Mandy came into the kitchen the following morning to find her dad reading the paper and drinking a cup of coffee. She raised her eyebrows. 'Shouldn't you be using your exercise machine?'

Mr Hope jumped rather guiltily to his feet. 'Well, you know, there's a busy morning ahead. I haven't really got time.'

Mandy fixed him with a stern look. 'You have to make time for exercise,' she informed him. 'Anyway, I thought that this machine was supposed to make exercise easy.'

'Hmm,' said Mr Hope. He pulled on his white coat. 'I think I'll just go and check the residential unit.' He hurried out of the door.

'I hope Tania's going to be in a good mood today,' James said when he arrived a bit later.

Mandy nodded. 'Me too. You didn't mind me asking her did you?'

James shook his head. 'It can't be much fun for her not having any friends here,' he said. 'Which shops should we go to first?' he asked, as they set off for Tania's house.

'How about Mr Cecil's chocolate shop?' Mandy suggested. 'I want to get Jean and Simon something from there.'

James nodded. They reached Willow Cottage and knocked on the door. Tania opened it. 'Hi,' she said with a shy smile. 'Come in. I'll just get my coat.' James and Mandy stepped into the hall.

'Hello,' said Sally Benster, coming through from the kitchen. 'So, Tania tells me that you're all off Christmas shopping.' Mandy and James nodded. 'Well, have fun,' Mrs Benster said as

Tania came running down the stairs with her coat.

The phone rang and Mrs Benster hurried to pick it up.

'Come on,' said Tania to Mandy and James. 'Let's go.'

'Tania!' Mrs Benster called, as they were halfway out of the door. 'Hang on a minute!' She beckoned her over. 'It's Dad.'

Tania's face darkened. 'I'm not speaking to him!'

'Tania,' Mrs Benster sighed. 'He wants to come and visit before Christmas – to bring your Christmas presents over.'

'I don't want any Christmas presents from him!' Tania exclaimed. 'I'm not going to see him!'

'Tania!'

'No!' Tania turned and ran out of the door. Mandy and James stood in the hallway, looking awkwardly after her. Mrs Benster covered the receiver. 'Sorry about that,' she said to them quickly. 'Look, have a nice time shopping. I'll sort this out with Tania when she gets back.'

Mandy and James caught up with Tania at the bottom of the garden. She was scowling fiercely and Mandy decided that it was better not even to try and talk about what had just happened. 'The bus stop's this way,' she said.

Once in the bus, Tania threw herself down in a seat and stared out of the window. Mandy hoped Tania wasn't going to be in a bad mood all day. She looked at James. 'So what are you getting for your mum?' she asked, trying to sound as normal as possible.

'A scarf,' he said. 'How about you?'

'I'm not sure yet, but I thought maybe some different kinds of aromatherapy oils.'

To Mandy's relief, as the bus journey passed and she and James talked, the angry look started to fade from Tania's face. By the time they reached Walton she was sharing ideas for presents with them.

'I can't think of anything to get my gran,' she said. 'She's impossible and she gives me really weird presents. Last year she gave me a brown and pink woolly hat and gloves and now, whenever I go to see her, I have to wear them!'

They set off round the shops. The streets had been decorated with tinsel and strings of Christmas lights. There were people bustling about everywhere and every shop they went into was playing cheery Christmas music. The festive atmosphere seemed to keep Tania in a good mood. The only dangerous moment was when Mandy and James started discussing the presents they were going to get for their dads.

Tania shook back her blonde hair. 'Well, I guess that's one good thing about my parents being divorced, I don't have to buy Dad a present.' Her tone was light but Mandy saw the barely suppressed emotion in her eyes.

'Aren't you going to get him anything?' James asked.

Tania shook her head. 'Nope. Why should I? If it hadn't been for him they would never have got divorced.' She saw their curious faces. 'He was always away on business. Mum says they grew apart.' She frowned. 'I know they could have made it work if they'd have tried harder. I think Dad just didn't want to. If he'd really cared he could have stayed at home more.'

Mandy had a feeling that things probably hadn't been that simple, but she certainly wasn't going to risk annoying Tania by saying anything.

Tania's mouth was set in a thin line. 'Dad's ruined everything for me,' she said angrily. 'He's ruined my life and I never want to speak to him again!'

'Umm, I think I'll just call in here,' muttered James as they passed the hardware shop.

Mandy thankfully followed him in. Tania's moods changed so quickly, it was difficult keeping up with her. But surely her father couldn't be as bad as she made out? Mandy had a feeling that it was just Tania's anger and not her real feelings speaking out.

By the time they got back on the bus they were all laden down with carrier bags full of presents. 'I'm going to wrap mine tonight,' Mandy said.

'I think I'll do mine this afternoon,' Tania said. She sighed. 'It's not as if I've got anything else to do.'

'What about coming with us to Imogen's?' James suggested.

Remembering Tania's reaction when she had seen Star two days before, Mandy was surprised when Tania said, 'OK.' She looked warningly at them. 'But I'm not helping with Star,' she said. 'She's Imogen's now.'

As the bus chugged along the moor road towards Welford, Mandy thought about Imogen. How would she react when she saw her cousin? She had been very upset after Tania had shouted at her and hadn't mentioned Tania's name since. Mandy crossed her fingers. She hoped everything would be all right.

When they arrived at the stables they found Imogen grooming Star with Mrs Parker Smythe rather helplessly holding a body brush in her manicured fingers. 'You do her tail, Mummy,' Imogen was saying.

Gabriel was tied up next to Star. As they came through the gate he turned and, pricking his tiny black ears, whinnied softly at them.

'Tania, darling!' Mrs Parker Smythe exclaimed. 'What a lovely surprise.'

Mandy looked at Imogen. The little girl was

staring at Tania with a mixture of fear and anger in her eyes.

'Look, who's here, Immi,' Mrs Parker Smythe said, turning to her daughter.

Imogen glared at Tania. 'Go away!'

Mrs Parker Smythe started in astonishment. 'Immi?'

'I don't want her here, Mummy. Tell her to go away!' Imogen pleaded.

Tania stood looking very awkward, and her face went red.

'Imogen, whatever's the matter with you?' Mrs Parker Smythe said. 'Now say hello to Tania nicely.'

'No!' Throwing down the brush she was holding, Imogen burst into tears and ran off.

'I'll go after her!' Mandy said quickly. She caught up with Imogen by the gate. Tears were running down the little girl's face.

'I don't want Tania here!' she sobbed. 'She thinks I shouldn't have Star. I hate her!'

Mandy put her arm round her. 'But she's your cousin, Immi.'

'I don't care!' Imogen sobbed.

'I know she shouted at you,' Mandy said. 'But she was upset.' She squeezed Imogen's arm. 'Come on, Immi. Imagine how you would feel if you had had to sell Star.' To her relief Imogen's sobs quietened down.

'Well, she's not going to help me with Star,' Imogen muttered at last.

'She won't,' Mandy said and she led Imogen back over to the others.

'Immi!' said Mrs Parker Smythe. 'Darling! How could you be so rude to Tania? Now say you're sorry.'

'Sorry,' Imogen muttered, not sounding as if she meant it. She turned to her mother. 'I want to ride!' she said. 'I want to ride Star in the paddock.'

While Mandy and James helped her to tack up Star and Mrs Parker Smythe helped Imogen find her hat and gloves, Tania stood on her own by Gabriel. She tried to ignore him but he wouldn't let her, constantly trying to pull towards her and get at her pockets. When she moved out of his reach he pawed his front hoof on the ground until, finally, she had to go and stand beside him to keep him quiet. He seemed determined to make Tania like him.

At last Star was ready and Imogen led her down to the paddock. James brought Gabriel down to the gate. Tania came to stand beside him. Her eyes were fixed on Imogen and Star.

'Are you going to be all right?' Mandy asked Imogen as she mounted and Star threw her head up. Imogen nodded.

'Be careful, Immi!' Mrs Parker Smythe called nervously, as Mandy let go of the reins and Star pranced off round the field. 'Oh dear, Star looks terribly lively,' she added.

Star jogged and pulled. Imogen kept her reins short and Star started to shake her head. Mandy glanced at Tania. Her eyes were agitated and suddenly, as if she couldn't bear to watch any longer, she turned and started adjusting Gabriel's rug. He nuzzled her affectionately. She smoothed his forelock out from underneath his headcollar. 'There's a good boy,' she murmured, her back to Imogen and Star. 'Good boy.'

Imogen walked and trotted Star round the paddock for fifteen minutes

'Maybe you could give Imogen some lessons, Tania?' Mrs Parker Smythe said as Imogen brought Star in.

'I don't need lessons, Mummy,' Imogen protested. 'I'm fine!'

Mrs Parker Smythe looked doubtful. 'I don't know. You didn't canter once. Maybe we should have got you a quieter pony.'

'No!' Imogen exclaimed. 'Star's perfect! I love her!'

'I know you do, sweetheart, but she is a bit of a handful.'

'I can cope!' Imogen turned to Mandy. 'I can, can't I, Mandy?'

Mandy nodded. 'I'm sure Star will settle down soon, Mrs Parker Smythe.'

Imogen's mum looked at Star with a worried expression on her face. 'Well, we'll see,' she said, not sounding convinced. 'Now turn Star out, Imogen, and come inside.'

Imogen and James led Star and Gabriel down to the paddock. Mandy swallowed. Surely Mrs Parker Smythe couldn't really be thinking about selling Star? It would break Imogen's heart. She caught sight of Tania watching the ponies being released into the field. She knew Tania's feelings about not helping with Star but this was really important. It could mean the difference between Star staying and being sold. She hurried over. 'Tania . . .' she began.

'No,' Tania said abruptly before Mandy had even asked the question. 'I'm not helping.'

'Why not?' Mandy demanded.

'I just can't!'

'But why?'

Tania glared at her. 'Just leave it, OK! I said no!' She strode off to stand at the paddock fence.

Mandy's heart sank. If Tania wouldn't help then she and James would have to think of something. And remembering the worried look on Mrs Parker Smythe's face, she had a feeling they were going to have to think of something fast!

Eight

'If Star is too much for Imogen, it might be better for her to be sold,' Mrs Hope said when Mandy confided the problem that evening.

'Mum!' said Mandy.

'You've got to be realistic, love. Imogen would probably be happier with a quieter pony,' Mrs Hope put out a cheese and onion quiche on the table.

'She wouldn't. She loves Star!' Mandy refused to believe that Imogen would be better off with a different pony. Yes, Star was lively but deep down Mandy was sure she was a loving, affectionate pony who just needed time to settle into her new home. She had behaved beautifully when Tania had stopped her running off down the road and had calmed her down.

Mandy hoped James would have some ideas of what they could do to help Imogen with Star, but when he arrived at Animal Ark the next morning he was also at a loss. 'I guess we've just got to make sure that Mrs Parker Smythe doesn't see her doing anything too naughty,' he said. 'And that she does settle down in time.'

Mandy agreed. 'If only Tania would step in.'

'Even if she would, do you think Imogen would accept her help?' James said. 'Tania isn't exactly her favourite person at the moment.'

Mandy sighed. She had to admit that James was right. *Oh, why is life never simple?* she thought.

To Mandy's surprise, Tania turned up at the stables that morning. 'I was bored,' she said by way of explanation. She sat on the fence and watched them start to groom Star and Gabriel. Imogen completely ignored her.

'You could help if you wanted,' Mandy suggested to Tania, as she picked up a body brush.

Tania shook her head. 'No thanks.' She watched James brushing out Gabriel's tail.

'You'll break the hairs like that,' she said as he dragged the brush through the tangles. 'Look, you do it like this.' Jumping off the fence she showed him how to untangle a few hairs at a time. 'It takes longer but it's worth it,' she told him.

'Thanks,' he said.

She moved round to Gabriel's head and patted him. 'You don't want broken hairs in your tail, do you?' she said gently to him, and Mandy saw her reach into her pocket and feed him a piece of carrot. Mandy raised her eyebrows slightly but knew better than to risk annoying Tania by making a comment.

Imogen fetched Star's tack. 'Will you help me, James?' she asked, holding out the bridle. As usual, Star started to shake her head as soon as James tried to put the bridle on. At last he got it over her ears and started to buckle up the straps. Star carried on shaking her head.

Tania frowned from the fence. 'The browband's too tight,' she said. The others turned and looked at her. She shrugged. 'It is. It's new, isn't it?'

Imogen nodded. The browband on the bridle was brand-new from the saddlers, made of leather and covered with smart blue and red velvet.

'Well, it's too tight,' said Tania. 'Star's got a broad forehead and needs a bigger browband than most ponies. Change it and she'll stop shaking her head as much.' She looked as if that was her final word.

'Have you got the old browband?' Mandy asked Imogen. She told them it was in the house, and hurried off to get it.

James held Star. She stamped her feet impatiently. 'It will help calm her down if you walk her around before you put the saddle on,' Tania said. 'I used to lunge her before getting on. It seems to settle her.'

Mandy felt exasperation fill her. 'For goodness sake, Tania. Why don't you just agree to help?'

Tania jumped off the fence and walked to the paddock gate. She stared out at the field, her face stormy.

Mandy only just managed to control her temper.

James touched her arm. 'Star's ready. Are you coming?'

Mandy nodded. They left Tania by the paddock gate and took Gabriel and Star out along the drive and up the hill. Having Gabriel walking alongside her seemed to calm Star down. Imogen was very happy. 'Star's being much better today,' she said, patting her pony's neck. 'Mummy should see her like this.'

When they got back to the stables, Gabriel lifted his head and whinnied to Tania. She turned from the gate, looking surprised and almost pleased. She came over. 'Hi,' she said. She patted the Miniature horse, who nudged her with his head. Her bad mood seemed to have vanished. 'How were they both?'

'Not too bad,' said Mandy.

'Do you want me to take him down to the field?' Tania asked James, who was holding Gabriel's leadrope.

'OK.' James nodded.

Mandy watched Tania lead Gabriel off and sighed to herself. Being with Tania was very wearing. You just never knew what mood she would be in. It was a bit like walking on eggshells, she thought, always going carefully, never knowing when she would crack.

Mandy, James and Tania walked back to the village together at lunch-time. Mrs Benster was in the garden of Willow Cottage, collecting some logs from a pile by the back door.

'Hi, Mum!' Tania called.

Mrs Benster smiled. 'What good timing. I've just made some mince pies. Would you like some?'

'Yes please,' Mandy and James said eagerly. They followed her into the house.

'Tania, something came for you in the post,' Mrs Benster said, handing round the mince pies. 'It's over there, on the side.'

Mandy saw that Tania looked suddenly suspicious. 'It's not from Dad is it?'

Mrs Benster sighed. 'No.'

Tania picked up the brown envelope and started to open it.

'What is it?' James asked, munching on a warm mince pie.

Tania pulled out a small cardboard folder from the envelope. 'Miniature horse Passport,' she read out. She quickly flicked through it. 'It's a passport for Gabriel.'

Mandy remembered. 'It must have been sent on by the delivery company,' she said. 'Dad said they had Gabe's passport there.' Tania handed it over to her and she looked through the pages. There was an identification page with a photograph of Gabriel and particulars such as his height, colour and a record of his breeding, a page showing his vaccinations and then a page recording the details of the owner. 'Look!' she said to Tania. 'It's got your name in!'

Tania looked. 'Owner: Tania Benster,' she read out. 'Address: Willow Cottage, 16 Walton Road, Welford.'

'Wow,' James said, looking over her shoulder. 'Doesn't it look good?'

For a long moment Tania stared down at the page and then she abruptly put the passport down. 'It will have to be changed,' she said. 'He's not mine.'

'Yes he is,' Mandy pointed out. 'It says so. You're his owner.'

'But I don't want to be,' said Tania, almost desperately. She pushed the passport away across the table and turned to her mum. 'You'll have to send it back and get it changed, Mum. Tell them he's not mine.'

'Well, we'll see . . .' Mrs Benster said.

'No, Mum! You will!'

Mrs Benster held up her hands. 'All right,' she said. 'I'm in no mood for an argument.' She went over to the kettle and turned it on. 'Your father's coming round tomorrow afternoon, Tania. He wants to see you.'

Tania stared in horror. 'No!'

'Yes,' Mrs Benster said. She looked firmly at her daughter. 'I said you'd be in.'

'Well, I won't be!' Tania exclaimed, her eyes blazing. 'I'm not going to see him. I hate him!' With that she stormed out of the room, slamming the door behind her.

There was a silence. Mandy glanced at Mrs Benster. Her face looked suddenly very tired. As if suddenly remembering that Mandy and James were there she turned to them. 'I'm sorry,' she said. 'I should have told Tania when she didn't have company.' She ran a hand across her forehead. 'Sometimes I think all my common sense has deserted me.'

Mandy stood up rather awkwardly. 'We better go,' she said.

James nodded. 'Can you tell Tania we'll see her tomorrow morning?'

Mrs Benster nodded and showed them to the door.

As Mandy and James cycled up to Beacon House the air froze their breath in great white clouds. It had turned much colder and they were very glad of their gloves and scarves.

'You better ride Star in the paddock today,' Mandy told Imogen. 'The road will be too icy.'

As Imogen mounted, Tania arrived. She came down to the paddock and leaned against the fence. Gabriel, who had been grazing, came over and nudged her hands hopefully. Have you bought me any treats today? he seemed to say.

'I'm going to canter Star,' Imogen told Mandy and James. 'Mummy thinks I'm too scared too but I'm going to show her that I'm not.'

She rode off. Mandy and James watched her trotting round. 'I don't know if cantering is such a good idea,' Mandy said to James.

Star was pulling hard but Imogen looked determined. After a few minutes, she grabbed hold of Star's mane, leaned forward, and kicked hard with her heels. Star leaped forward, throwing her head between her knees and pulling the reins free from Imogen's hands. With a frightened cry Imogen tumbled from the saddle. For one awful moment there was a tangle of legs and arms and hooves, and then Imogen was lying on the grass and Star was cantering away.

'Quick!' Mandy gasped to James.

They scrambled over the gate and started racing across the field. To her relief, Mandy saw Imogen starting to sit up. But her relief was short-lived. A high-pitched shriek rang out behind them. Mandy glanced round. Mrs Parker Smythe was standing at the paddock gate, her eyes wide with horror.

Imogen stood up. She looked shaky but appeared to be all in one piece.

'Are you all right?' James gasped.

Imogen nodded. 'I fell off,' she said rather dazedly.

'We saw,' said James.

'And so did your mum,' said Mandy in dismay, seeing Mrs Parker Smythe running across the field towards them.

Mrs Parker Smythe reached them and clasped Imogen in her arms. 'Oh, Immi, are you all right, sweetheart?' she exclaimed.

'I'm fine, Mummy.' Imogen. said, trying to wriggle out of her mother's embrace. 'I just fell off, that's all.'

'Just fell off! I saw what that pony did. I was watching from the house. That's it, Immi. Enough's enough. That pony has to go!'

'No!' Imogen cried, aghast.

'Yes,' Mrs Parker Smythe said firmly. 'I'm not having you risking your neck. Star needs a more experienced rider and you need a pony you can take out on rides and canter round on and jump. Star's too lively.'

'But I love her!' wailed Imogen.

'I won't hear another word on the subject!' Mrs Parker Smythe said.

'I hate you!' Imogen cried, her face crumpling, and then, turning, she ran across the field towards the house. Mrs Parker Smythe hurried after her.

'Well,' said James in a stunned voice. 'Poor Imogen.'

Mandy turned to Tania who was standing a little way off, holding Star. 'Tania,' she pleaded. 'You've got to help. You heard what your aunt said. She's going to sell Star. If you say you'll help Imogen she might change her mind.'

Tania's lip trembled. 'I can't.'

'You can!' Mandy exclaimed, but Tania shook her head stubbornly. It was too much for Mandy. She lost her temper. 'For goodness sake, will you stop being so selfish?' she cried. 'Why don't you try thinking about someone other than yourself for a change?' She saw the shock on Tania's face but went on regardless, her anger with Tania fuelled by her concern for Imogen and Star and her pent-up frustration. 'You don't think about anyone else's feelings. Everyone's going out of their way to be nice to you but you don't care about anyone but yourself.'

Tania drew herself up, her eyes blazing fiercely. 'And I suppose you know what it's like to have parents who are divorced, do you?'

'No I don't!' Mandy exclaimed equally fiercely. 'But I do know that it doesn't give you the right to go around hurting other people.' With that, she grabbed Star from Tania and marched towards the gate.

'Mandy!' James said, hurrying after her, sounding shocked. 'Calm down.'

She shook his hand off her arm and strode on, but it wasn't long before her temper began to cool. By the time she reached the gate her hands were starting to tremble. *Oh no*, she thought. *What have I done?* She fumbled with the bolt.

James pulled back the gate for her. But just as Mandy started to lead Star through they heard a sob. They turned round. Tania had collapsed into a heap on the ground and was crying into her hands.

James glanced at Mandy with worried eyes. 'What should we do?'

Mandy swallowed. 'Go back.' It was the only thing they could do.

James nodded. With a nervous feeling in the pit of her stomach, Mandy started to walk Star slowly back across the field towards Tania.

'Look!' James whispered suddenly.

Gabriel was walking towards Tania. He stopped beside her and then started nuzzling at her hair. Tania tried to push him away. 'Go away!' she gulped but Gabriel wouldn't leave. He nuzzled her face and hands. His affection was too much for Tania. A loud sob tore from her. 'Oh, Gabe!' she cried, putting her arms round him. 'No one understands. No one cares.'

Mandy suddenly felt dreadful. She took a step forward. 'Tania?' Tania jumped and looked up. For a moment the two girls just stared at each other then Mandy took a deep breath. 'I'm sorry,' she said. 'I . . . I shouldn't have said those things.'

For a moment, Mandy thought that Tania was going to explode at her again but then suddenly she bit her lip, and a tear trickled down her cheek. 'No, I'm the one that should be sorry,' she whispered, her voice catching. 'I have been selfish. I know I have.' She brushed her tears away with the back of her hand. 'It's just so hard not to be.' Her voice took on a note of despair. 'It feels like no one cares.'

'Gabe cares,' James said quietly, looking at the little horse who was nuzzling Tania.

Tania touched Gabriel's nose. His lips nibbled gently at her fingers.

'It doesn't matter how many times you push him away,' Mandy said. 'He'll always come back. That's the good thing about animals. They're always there for you.'

James nodded. 'They love you, no matter what.'

Tania looked at Gabe. 'He's yours,' Mandy said to her. 'And he loves you.'

Tania's eyes looked panicky. 'But I don't want him to love me,' she said.

Mandy understood. 'In case you lose him?'

Tania nodded.

'But that won't happen,' Mandy kneeled down beside her. 'Don't you understand? You're his owner, Tania. It says so on the passport. No one can take him away from you. He's yours.' She looked pleadingly at the other girl. 'He'll love you so much if you just give him a chance.'

As if he agreed, Gabriel snorted gently and nuzzled Tania's hair. Mandy saw Tania's face melt. 'Oh, Gabe,' she whispered and she flung her arms round his neck again. Tears coursed down her cheeks. 'You *are* mine, aren't you? All mine!'

Mandy looked at James in relief.

At last, Tania stood up. There were still traces of tears on her face but her eyes were brave. 'I'm going to tell Auntie Sonia that I'll help with Star,' she said. 'You're right. I have been selfish. But not any more.'

'Tania!' cried Mandy 'That's great! I'm sure if you offer to help, Imogen will be allowed to keep her.'

Tania took a deep breath and looked at Star. 'It'll be hard,' she said. 'I do still love her. But she'll be happy with Imogen.' She put her hand on Gabriel's neck. 'And I've got Gabriel now.' She looked towards the Parker Smythes' house. 'Right, here goes!'

'Maybe you should let your aunt calm down a little first,' James suggested.

Mandy nodded, remembering Mrs Parker Smythe's horrified face. 'We could come back after lunch,' she said. 'We don't want to ask her when she's still really upset, she might say no.'

Tania saw the sense in what they were saying. 'OK,' she said. 'But straight after lunch.'

They went back to Tania's house for lunch. She showed them round the back garden. It wasn't huge but it was securely fenced in with two solid-looking sheds. 'This will be perfect for Gabe,' Mandy said.

'One shed for him to shelter in and one for his feed and bedding,' said Tania. 'And I'll take him up to visit Star lots so they can still stay friends.'

Tania showed them her bedroom. It had bare white walls and most of her things were still in boxes. Tania went happily to the window. 'I'll be able to see Gabe from here.' She looked round the room. 'I guess I should really start putting some of my posters up and unpacking my things.'

Mandy smiled. She hoped that it was a sign that Tania was finally starting to accept that her life had changed.

After grabbing a sandwich they hurried back up the hill eager to find Mrs Parker Smythe and Imogen. It was getting very cold and by the time they reached Beacon House they all had bright red cheeks and noses.

'It's going to snow!' said Mandy, looking at the sky. 'I bet it's going to snow.'

'We can go sledging,' James said. 'Do you like sledging?' he asked Tania.

'I love it,' she replied. 'But I haven't got a sledge.'

'You can share ours then,' James said.

'Thanks!' Tania looked really pleased. She reached for the doorbell. 'Well, here goes,' she said. They stamped their feet in the cold as they waited for someone to answer. The housekeeper, Mrs Bates, eventually opened the door.

'Hi, Mrs Bates,' Tania said. 'We're looking for Auntie Sonia.'

'She's popped out,' the housekeeper told them.

'Oh.' Tania's face fell. 'Is Imogen here then?' she asked.

Mrs Bates shook her head. 'No, she went out to the stables about half an hour ago.'

'Oh right,' said Tania. 'Well OK, we'll go and find her there.'

They went round to the stables. 'Imogen!' Tania called out.

There was no answer. They checked the stables and then walked down to the field. Gabriel was standing by the gate. 'Where's Star?' Mandy asked in surprise. The two ponies were normally always together.

'Mandy!' said James, looking round the field. 'She's not here!'

Mandy frowned. 'But she's got to be!'

'Let's check the tack room,' Tania said. They ran to the tack room. Star's saddle and bridle were gone. In their place was a note.

'Dear Mummy,' Mandy read out, grabbing it. 'I have taken Star out for a ride. I want to show you that I can. She is safe, really she is. See you later.' Mandy looked up. 'Love, Imogen.'

'Oh, no,' Tania whispered. 'What if she falls off again?'

'And this time really hurts herself,' said James.

'We've got to find her,' Mandy said, throwing down the note. 'Before it's too late.'

Nine

They ran as fast as they could down the drive. 'She must have gone up towards High Cross!' James panted. 'We would have seen her if she'd been coming down the hill.'

Mandy slid and almost fell as she stepped on a patch of ice. Her heart lurched. What if Star was to slip and stumble? She felt sick to the stomach thinking of the lively pony and of Imogen, the inexperienced rider.

Tania suddenly stopped dead. Mandy and James almost ran into her. 'Listen!' she exclaimed.

Mandy heard a faint clatter of hooves. It got louder and louder. 'Star!' she gasped as the palomino pony came cantering down the drive towards them. She was riderless, her reins flapping round her legs.

Tania leaped in front of her. 'Whoa!' The pony skidded to a halt and Tania grabbed her reins, her face pale. 'Imogen must have fallen off,' she said.

'We've got to find her!' said Mandy. 'She might be hurt and it's so cold.' As she spoke the first few flakes of snow started to fall.

Tania seemed to make up her mind. Putting her foot in the stirrup she mounted the excited pony. Star shook her head and twirled on the spot.

'What are you doing?' Mandy cried, as Tania turned the pony back down the drive.

'Going to find Imogen. It'll be quicker this way. I can retrace her tracks.'

'But . . .'

Tania didn't listen. She kicked her heels into Star's side and the pony galloped away, keeping to the grass at the side of the drive.

'Oh no!' gasped Mandy to James. 'Look!'

Mrs Parker Smythe's sleek silver car was turning in through the gates. Mrs Parker Smythe slammed her brakes on to avoid Star and jumped out of the car. 'Tania! What are you doing?'

Tania galloped past without replying. Mandy and James ran up to Mrs Parker Smythe. 'What on earth's going on?' Mrs Parker Smythe demanded. 'Whatever is Tania—'

Mandy interrupted her with a hurried explanation. 'Imogen's taken Star out. We think she must have fallen off somewhere. Tania's gone to find her.'

Mrs Parker Smythe stared at her uncomprehendingly. 'Imogen took Star out on a ride? On her own?'

'Yes! There's a note in the tack room. She said she wanted to prove to you that she could.' Mandy made a split-second decision to tell Mrs Parker Smythe everything.

As the words sank in, Mandy saw Mrs Parker Smythe go pale. 'Oh my goodness,' she whispered.

'We're got to help Tania look for Imogen,' said Mandy. 'Now!'

She ran out of the gate, ignoring Mrs Parker Smythe's cry of 'Wait!'

'This way,' said James turning up the hill. They ran past Upper Welford Hall and past the drive to High Cross Farm. Snowflakes swirled towards them and their feet slipped on the road. Every so often there was a set of hoofprints on the grass at the side of the road but they were rapidly becoming covered by a dusting of white.

'Which way now?' gasped James, as the road ended by forking into two rough tracks. One led up to the Beacon. One went round the side of the mountain and into Piper's Wood.

'This way!' said Mandy, spotting a trail of hoofprints. She ran along the narrow track, pushing branches out of the way, tripping over concealed tree roots. The mud under the trees was so churned up that it was soon impossible to follow the hoofprints any further. She stopped and looked round. What now? Paths led off in different directions, and the only sound was their gasping for breath. The snow was getting heavier now.

'Imogen!' James called. 'Tania!'

His voice was loud in the eerie silence of the cold wood.

'Imogen!' Mandy shouted as loud as she could.

There was no reply. 'Come on, we can't just wait here,' Mandy said, setting off down the widest of the tracks.

They walked down the path, taking it in turns to shout out Imogen's name. Suddenly James gasped Mandy's arm. 'Listen!'

There was an answering shout and then Tania came trotting through the trees. 'Have you found her?' Mandy gasped as Tania dismounted.

Tania shook her head. 'No. I lost the trail.' She looked round at the dark trees, her eyes desperate. 'She could be anywhere.'

'We'll find her,' Mandy said. 'Come on!' They set off down the path again.

Tania led Star. 'If only she could help us,' she said as they reached a clearing and were faced with another four different tracks.

Mandy looked at Star. The pony's ears were pricked. 'Maybe she can!' she said. 'Look at her! She's looking down that path.'

'She might just have heard something,' said Tania.

'Come on.' James made the decision. 'Let's go that way!'

'Imogen! Imogen!' they shouted, as they stamped along. Suddenly they heard a faint cry.

'That's her!' gasped Tania. 'Come on!' They hurried along the path. Calling out, they received an answering cry.

'We're closer!' said Mandy. They ran round a bend in the track and stopped. There was Imogen. She was huddled underneath an oak tree, tears streaming down her face. Snow had settled all around her.

'Oh, Immi!' cried Tania, flinging Star's reins at James and racing over to her cousin. 'Are you all right?' Dropping to her knees she wrapped her arms tightly round Imogen. 'There, there. Don't cry. We're here now.'

For a long moment Imogen just clung on to Tania. Tears streamed down both their faces. 'We've been so worried,' said Tania.

'What happened, Imogen? Are you all right?' Mandy asked, kneeling down in the snow beside her.

Imogen took a deep gulping breath. 'Star ran away with me. Something frightened her when we came into the wood and she just took off. I tried to stay on. It was horrible. There were branches hitting me and then she stumbled and I lost my grip. I . . . I've hurt my ankle.' Her voice rose. 'And now Mummy's never going to let me keep Star!'

'She will,' Tania said firmly. 'I'm going to tell her I'll help you, Imogen. I'll come each day.'

'Really?' said Imogen her face lighting up, full of hope.

'Really,' said Tania. She hugged Imogen. 'I'm sorry I've been horrid. But I'll help you from now on, I promise. I'll show you how to get Star to canter and teach you how to jump. And when you're really good,' she smiled, 'Gabe and I will come and watch you at all the horse shows you're going to enter.'

Imogen smiled happily. 'I'd like that.'

'Good,' said Tania. She looked rather anxiously at Mandy. 'But first we have to get you home.'

'Let me have a look at your ankle,' Mandy said. She tried to help Imogen off with her boot but the pain was too great for the little girl and she screamed. 'We'd better leave it,' Mandy said. 'We need to get you back as quickly as possible.'

'But I can't walk,' said Imogen.

'You can sit on Star and we'll lead you,' Mandy replied.

Looking slightly scared but with her mouth set in determined line, Imogen let Mandy and James help her on to Star's back. Her ankle knocked against the saddle and she gasped and went pale. For one horrid moment Mandy thought she was going to faint.

'You're being very brave,' she told Imogen. 'Now come on, it won't be long before you're home.'

They set off slowly down the path with Tania

leading Star and Mandy and James walking on either side. Mandy looked anxiously at Imogen. She was starting to shiver. Mandy shrugged off her jacket. 'Here,' she said. 'Put this on, Imogen.'

'But you'll get cold,' Imogen said.

'No I won't. I'm going to run ahead and try and get help,' said Mandy. She looked at Tania and James who both nodded. 'See you later!' Mandy called, heading off into the trees.

She ran as fast as she could, her heart pounding in her throat, her breath coming in great gasps. At last she reached Beacon House and banged on the door.

'Mandy!' cried Mrs Parker Smythe, opening it almost immediately. 'Where's Imogen? Have you found her?'

'Yes!' Mandy gasped struggling for breath. 'She's in the woods. She's hurt her ankle. James and Tania are with her.'

Just then there was the sound of a car driving up behind her. Mandy turned. 'Dad!' she cried, seeing her father's Land-rover.

Mr Hope leaped out. 'I came as soon as I could,' he said to Mrs Parker Smythe. He turned to Mandy. 'What's happened? Have you found Imogen?'

'She's in the woods, with James and Tania.

She's hurt her ankle,' Mandy said. 'I said I'd get help.'

'OK, let's go,' said Mr Hope.

'Thank you so much for coming, Mr Hope,' said Mrs Parker Smythe, as they drove up the road in the Land-rover. 'I just didn't know who else to call. My husband is away on business.'

'No problem,' said Mr Hope, his eyes fixed on the snowy road. 'Right, here we are.'

Just as they threw open the doors of the Land-rover, Tania and James appeared leading Imogen on Star.

'Immi!' cried Mrs Parker Smythe.

'Mummy!' Imogen cried and then she fainted.

'I don't think it's broken,' said Mr Hope a little while later, looking up from examining Imogen's ankle. It was so swollen that it had been necessary to cut through her riding boot to get it off. 'I think it's just a bad sprain but you should visit the Cottage Hospital just in case. I'll bandage it up until you get there.'

Mandy, James and Tania were sitting on towels on an enormous sofa. Everything in the Parker Smythe's house seemed to be white and gold and Mandy was very conscious of her muddy jeans.

Imogen was wrapped in a duvet, with a cup of hot chocolate in her hands. Although she was safely back home she still looked anxious.

As Mr Hope set to work, Mrs Parker looked gratefully at him. 'Thank you so much, Adam.'

Mr Hope secured the bandage. 'No problem,' he said.

'I just don't understand why you did it, Immi,' Mrs Parker Smythe said, turning to her daughter.

'Because you said you were going to sell Star. I wanted to show you that she was safe to ride!' Imogen replied.

'Well, she obviously isn't,' said Mrs Parker Smythe. 'She is going to have to go.'

'No, Mummy!'

'Auntie Sonia,' Tania broke in. 'What about if I helped Immi? I could come here each day.'

Mrs Parker Smythe shook her head. 'Star's just too lively, Tania. I think Imogen needs a quieter pony.'

'But I want Star!' Imogen cried.

'Star's fine,' Tania protested. 'She's only lively when you first get on. If I ride her each day before Imogen then she'll be as quiet as anything.'

'But what if you're not here, Tania?'

'Well, I can show Imogen how to use a lunge

rope,' Tania said. 'That would work just as well. But I will be here. I promise I'll come every day.'

'We'll share her,' Imogen said. 'Like I share Button and Barney with John. Only it will be better because we'll look after her together and Tania won't have to go away to school like John does.' She turned to Tania. 'You can teach me how to jump.'

Tania smiled. 'And you can help me look after Gabe.'

Mrs Parker Smythe started. 'You've decided you want to keep Gabriel?' she said.

Tania nodded. 'Thank you for buying him for me. I'm sorry I've been so horrible.' She got up and hugged her aunt. 'He's the best present I could ever have.'

'Well, goodness,' Mrs Parker Smythe said, going rather pink but hugging Tania back. 'This is a surprise. What made you change your mind?'

Tania grinned at Mandy and James. 'Oh, just an argument I had.'

'An argument? Really, Tania, darling, you do talk in riddles some of the time!'

Tania looked at her aunt. 'You will let Imogen keep Star won't you?' she pleaded. 'I really do promise I'll help and I'll never let Imogen do anything dangerous and after all, Star did help us find Imogen. She showed us the right track to take in the woods.'

'Please, Mummy!' Imogen said. 'If it hadn't been for Star I might still be there now!'

Mrs Parker Smythe looked from one to the other and then nodded. 'All right then.'

'Oh, thank you, Mummy!' cried Imogen, Mandy breathed a huge sigh of relief.

'Now, young lady,' Mr Hope said to Imogen. 'it's time to get you to the hospital.' He bent down to pick her up.

'Please can I see Star and Gabriel before I go?' Imogen begged.

Mr Hope looked at Mrs Parker Smythe, who nodded. 'But not until you've put another coat on and gloves and a hat,' she said.

When Imogen was kitted out to her mother's satisfaction, Mr Hope lifted her up in his strong arms and carried her down to the stable. The snow had stopped falling and lay in a perfect white layer.

Star was in her loose box and Gabriel was in the shelter in the field. 'I'll bring him in,' Tania said quickly. 'It's too cold for him out there. He'd better stay in a stable tonight and then tomorrow I'll take him down to my house.'

'But you will bring him back lots, won't you?' Imogen asked.

Tania nodded. 'I promise.'

As she went to fetch him, everyone else gathered around Star's stable door. Imogen stroked her gently on the nose. 'I love you, Star,' she whispered.

Just then there was the sound of a car arriving. Mrs Parker Smythe looked up in surprise. 'Who can that be?' she said. A tall man and a blonde woman came round the side of the house.

'It's Tania's mum!' said James.

'Sally!' exclaimed Mrs Parker Smythe. Her tone changed slightly. 'And . . . um . . . Richard.'

Sally Benster looked round at everyone. 'Hello,' she said. 'We're looking for Tania.' She frowned. 'She was supposed to be back at Willow Cottage.'

Mandy looked at the man beside Mrs Benster and her eyes suddenly widened as she remembered Mrs Benster warning Tania that she wanted her to be at home that afternoon. Could this man be . . .

'Dad!' Everyone turned. Tania stood a little way off with Gabriel. She was staring at the man, her face pale.

Her father took a step forward. 'Tania.'

Tension hung in the freezing air as Tania and her father stared at each other. For a moment no one moved and then Gabe, curious as always, pulled forward to meet the stranger. Slipping on the snow, Tania let go of the leadrope. Gabe trotted over. 'Nice pony,' Mr Benster said.

Mandy saw Tania swallow. 'He's mine and he's not a pony, he's a Miniature horse.' She clicked her tongue. 'Gabe!' The little horse looked round and then trotted back to her. She put her hand on his neck. 'He's all mine.' Her voice shook slightly on the last words as she stared almost defiantly at her father.

Gabriel stepped towards Mr Benster.

'Gabe!' Tania called.

The little horse stopped and looked round at her. He pricked his ears as if to say, Well, what are you waiting for?

Tania looked at her dad and suddenly caught her breath in a sob.

'Tania,' Mr Benster said in concern.

The next instant Tania was in her father's arms. 'Oh, Dad!' she cried, her shoulders shaking as he pulled her close. Not wanting to be left out, Gabe tried to push in on the action.

Tania started to half laugh and half cry. 'Oh, Gabe, I do love you! And, Dad, I love you too!'

'I love you too, sweetheart,' said Mr Benster, hugging her as if he was never going to let her go. 'No matter what happens. I always will!'

Mandy saw Mrs Benster watching from a distance, tears spilling down her cheeks.

Oh Gabe, Mandy thought. *You really are a wonderful horse.*

She felt her father touch her arm. 'I think we might leave the Bensters here and get Imogen to the hospital,' he said quietly. 'OK?'

Mandy nodded. 'OK,' she said with a happy smile.

The Ambassador
of
Good Will

Ten

The next morning, when Mandy woke up at the usual time, her room felt colder and darker than normal and there was a curious stillness that hung in the air. She sat up quickly. The snow! How deep was it now?

Jumping out of bed, she raced to the window. 'Oh, wow!' she gasped. Although the light was dim and grey, she could see that everything was covered in a thick, snowy blanket. The wheelbarrow in the garden, the flower-beds, the bird table, the trees – everything was white.

Mandy felt her toes start to tingle with the cold. Excitement bubbled up in her. It had snowed and it was Christmas Eve! Pulling on some clothes, she hurried downstairs and went outside. The garden stretched out before her, an expanse of perfect whiteness. Mandy raced across it leaving great snowy footprints. She stopped and grinned as she decided to test the snow by making a snowball.

Hearing the slight crunch of a footstep behind her, she turned round just in time to duck as a snowball whistled past her ear. Mr Hope was standing by the back door, another snowball already in his hands.

'*Dad!*' Mandy threw the snowball she was holding at him. Two minutes later, snowballs were flying back and forth across the garden and the still air was shattered by shrieks and shouts.

'Stop! Stop! I've got snow down my wellies!' Mandy exclaimed at last.

'Count yourself lucky – it's down my neck!' Mr Hope replied. Dusting off his hands he came over and put his arm round her. 'Snow for Christmas then.'

Mandy nodded. 'We can go sledging!'

'It doesn't look like much else will be happening today,' Mr Hope said, opening the side gate and looking at the snow that covered the drive. 'It's not going to be easy to get out in this.'

Mandy suddenly remembered. 'But James and I were supposed to be helping Tania with Gabe,' she said. 'We were going to take him down to Willow Cottage.'

'You'll find it difficult getting to Tania's in this,' Mr Hope said. 'You'll have to wait until the roads have been cleared.'

'I guess so.' Mandy felt disappointed. She had been looking forward to seeing Gabriel finally settled into Tania's back garden.

Mrs Hope was already cooking breakfast as they went into the kitchen. She smiled as they came in, shaking the snow off their clothes. 'You look like snowmen!' she said. 'Now who's for scrambled eggs on toast?'

Mr Hope sighed happily. 'Double helpings please!'

As Mandy watched her father tuck into an enormous plateful of fluffy scrambled eggs she grinned. 'Seeing as you'll be stuck around here today, Dad, you'll be able to spend lots of time on your exercise machine!'

Mr Hope froze with a mouthful of scrambled eggs halfway to his mouth.

'That's an excellent idea, Mandy,' Mrs Hope said approvingly. She looked at Mr Hope. 'After all, Adam, you have been saying that the only reason you haven't been using it is because we've been so busy. Well, now's your chance.'

Mr Hope coughed. 'Well, you know the surgery could do with a tidy up.'

'I'll do that,' said Mandy helpfully.

'And the shelves could do with sorting out.'

'I'll do that as well,' Mandy said

Mr Hope thought for a moment. 'There's all the paperwork,' he said.

'Leave it for Jean,' said Mrs Hope. 'This is beginning to sound suspiciously like a list of excuses,' she said, her green eyes twinkling as she tucked a strand of hair behind her left ear and looked at Mr Hope.

'Dad!' said Mandy, pretending to sound shocked. 'Surely you're not going to tell us that you are trying to get out of using your brand-new exercise machine? The machine that makes exercising effortless and easy.'

Mr Hope gave up the pretence. 'It lied,' he said.

'Poor Dad,' Mandy said, putting her arm round him. 'But you know what they say. No pain, no gain. Now come on, let's get you into that tracksuit . . .'

Mr Hope was about to get up when his face suddenly brightened. 'But I can't exercise straight after breakfast, can I?' He shook his head. 'It could be dangerous.' He sat back firmly in his chair. 'No, no, no. I'd better just sit here and read this magazine until my breakfast has been digested.' He picked up his magazine with a contented sigh. 'Are there any more eggs?' he asked, looking up hopefully.

By mid morning, Mandy had tidied the surgery and cleaned out and fed her rabbits and the animals in the residential unit. There didn't seem much else to do. The driveway and road were still far too deep in snow for her to go out.

She finished wrapping her Christmas presents and then rang Tania. There was no reply from Willow Cottage. She rang James to find that he was snowed in as well.

'Blackie loves it!' he said. 'He's been racing round the garden all morning.'

They arranged to go sledging as soon as the snow had cleared a bit. Mandy put down the phone and sighed. Although it was brilliant that it had snowed, it wasn't much fun on her own.

She decided to go and check the drive again to see if the snow had melted at all. She pulled on her wellies and went outside. As she shut the door she suddenly heard a faint noise and stopped to listen. It sounded like the tinkling of tiny bells. She frowned. What could it be? It seemed to be coming from down the drive and it was getting louder. She waded through the snow and suddenly gasped in amazement. There, coming up the hill, were Tania and Gabriel. The Miniature horse was pulling a red sledge and sitting on it was Imogen.

'Mandy!' the little girl cried, waving wildly.

'Hi!' called out Tania, who was almost up to the top of her boots in snow but was grinning broadly.

'What are you doing here?' Mandy cried in

delight as they reached her. Imogen was covered in rugs and blankets and Tania was muffled in a thick coat and gloves. Gabe had tinsel round his browband and his harness was covered in lots and lots of tiny Christmas bells.

'We've come to give you this,' said Imogen, holding out a brightly-wrapped present. 'It's from us for you. Well, from Tania really.'

'We really wanted to see you,' said Tania. 'And we thought it would be a fun thing to get Gabe to pull Imogen's sledge.' She smiled lovingly down at the little horse. 'He's brilliant at it and he hasn't had any trouble getting through the snow – he's as steady as anything.'

Mandy grinned at her. 'So he's not just a useless Miniature horse, then?'

Tania looked rather embarrassed. 'I can't believe I was ever so stupid.' She took the present from Imogen. 'I brought you this to say thank you for making me realise how wonderful Gabe is.'

Mandy took the present. It was a long thin cylinder. 'Open it!' said Imogen. 'Open it now.'

She looked inquiringly at Tania, who nodded. 'Yes, go on.'

Mandy peeled off her gloves so she could undo the sellotape, and then finally got the paper off and drew out a long, rolled-up tube. She unrolled it and gasped. It was an enormous poster of a spotted Miniature horse, just like Gabriel, with a thick, fluffy mane and tail and large, intelligent eyes. At the bottom of the poster were the words: *The Ambassador of Goodwill.*

'Happy Christmas!' said Tania.

'Do you like it?' Imogen demanded.

'I love it,' Mandy said, grinning from ear to ear. She already knew where it was going to go – right above her bed!

'Auntie Sonia gave it to me for my birthday to go with Gabe,' Tania explained. 'It's a picture of Gabriel's father. But I want you to have it. It's to say thank you for making me realise how wonderful Gabe is.' She met Mandy's eyes. 'As long as I've got Gabe, I know I can cope with anything.'

'And you'll always have Gabe,' Mandy said softly, looking at the little horse.

Tania nodded. 'Animals are for ever,' she said. She put her arms round Gabe's neck and hugged him fiercely. 'He's my horse and I am never, ever going to let him go.'

Gabriel tossed his head, his dark eyes peeping at Mandy from under Tania's arm. That suits me just fine, he seemed to say.

Mandy smiled. 'How's your Dad, Tania?'

'Fine,' Tania said with a happy smile. 'He stayed for a bit last night but then went home because he was worried about the snow. I'm going to go and visit him. He's even said I can bring Gabe with me. He can stay in Star's old stable and paddock and I'll be able see all my old friends.'

Just then the front door opened. 'Tania! Imogen!' Mrs Hope said. 'Goodness, how did you get here through all this snow?'

'Gabe pulled me,' Imogen said.

'Well, come in and have a hot drink and a mince pie,' Mrs Hope said. 'You must be freezing.'

'What about Gabe?' Tania asked. 'It'll be too cold for him to wait out here.'

Mandy looked at her mum. 'He could come into the kitchen, Mum,' she said, her eyes pleading. 'Just this once.'

Mrs Hope hesitated and then gave in. 'All right,' she said with a smile. 'I suppose it *is* Christmas, after all!'

They helped Imogen off the sledge and, with lots of chattering and laughing, led Gabe inside. He stood by the kitchen table, looking rather surprised as Mrs Hope handed out mugs of hot chocolate and mince pies. 'Happy Christmas, everyone,' she said.

Mandy fetched a plastic bowl and filled it with carrots. Gabe's tiny black ears pricked and he raised his head. She carried it over to him.

'Happy Christmas, Gabe!' she said.

Her eyes met Tania's and they both smiled.

LUCY DANIELS

Animal Ark™

Fox in the Frost

Illustrations by Jenny Gregory

Special thanks to Jenny Oldfield
Thanks also to C.J. Hall, B.Vet.Med., M.R.C.V.S., for reviewing
the veterinary material contained in this book.

Text copyright © 1997 Working Partners Limited
Created by Ben M. Baglio, London WC1X 9HH
Illustrations copyright © 1997 Jenny Gregory

First published as a single volume in Great Britain in 1997
by Hodder Children's Books

This bind-up edition published in 2008 by Hodder Children's Books

One

'Blackie, come back here!' James Hunter shouted. The black Labrador ignored him.

'That's a very obedient dog you have there.' Mandy Hope grinned. She clipped a sprig of holly from a thick bush by the roadside. They were out on the moortop, close to the Beacon, gathering holly for Christmas. The hillside was covered in white frost that sparkled in the sun.

'Blackie!' James jumped over a gate and careered after him, down the track to High Cross Farm.

'So well-trained, so reliable!'

'Yeah, yeah!' James's voice carried on the wind, before he vanished between the high stone walls.

Mandy reached higher. There was a sprig laden with shiny red berries. It would look great over the doorway at Animal Ark. She wanted the waiting-room to be bright and cheerful in the run-up to the festive season. But she reached too far. Her fingertips missed the branch and the frosty ground was slippy. 'Aagh!' Her arms whirled and she tipped forward.

Blackie heard her cry and came galloping back across the field.

'Blackie, where are you?' James's faint voice called.

'He's here!' Mandy was in the ditch. The dog's black nose snuffled her cheek. He butted her and licked the frost from her face. 'Ouch!' She gave up trying to fend him off. 'Ouch! Ouch!'

'What are you doing down there?' James peered over the wall, his face red from running.

'Ouch! These holly leaves are sharp!' Mandy's hat fell over her eyes as Blackie wrestled with her. 'Get him off me, James. I'm getting prickled to death!'

'Here, boy!' It was James's turn to grin. He climbed the wall and tried to tug the dog away. 'Sorry, Mandy, he thinks you want to play!'

'Well, I don't. Ouch! Get off, Blackie!' At last

Mandy struggled to her feet. The seat of her trousers was covered in frost and dead holly leaves. Her hat finally fell off as she bent to brush herself down.

Another game! Blackie seized the red woollen hat and charged up the hill towards Upper Welford Hall.

Mandy groaned. 'OK, I know it serves me right for being rude about him.' She sighed.

'Come on, we'd better get him back before he decides to invade the Hall gardens.' James set off after Blackie.

'Yep, Mr Western would really love that!' The owner of Upper Welford Hall would be furious with anyone who even so much as touched his smooth lawns and perfect flower-beds. Christmas or no Christmas, he would be phoning their mums and dads – if not the police – to complain.

'Uh-oh, I've lost him.' James came to a halt by the big double gates. 'Did you see which way he went?'

Mandy stumbled into James. 'No!' she gasped. She turned full circle, taking in the sweep of the white hillside, the tiny houses of Welford nestled in the valley, the shining river as it snaked its way through. 'But he can't have disappeared!'

James bent to peer under a hedge. 'Blackie!' he whispered. 'Look, Mandy, there's your hat!' He crawled along the hedge bottom and reached out for it. When he stood up, he looked worried. 'His footprints go right across the lawn!'

'Where to?' Mandy stared at the blank windows and closed doors of the lovely old hall. She prayed that Mr Western was out.

'I can't see. Wait, what was that?'

They heard an odd noise, somewhere between a squawk and cackle. The annoyed alarm call of a bird. 'It sounds like Blackie's found something else to chase.'

This time James groaned. 'Pheasants!'

They watched as a pair of russet-brown birds scuttled out of the opposite hedge and across Mr Western's flower-beds. Their dark heads gleamed and their long tail feathers skimmed the frosty earth.

'Oh, Blackie!' Mandy was disappointed in him. James's dog was lively, but not usually so much trouble. Now the birds broke into a run and began to flap their wings. They clattered and whirred as they took flight.

'Woof!' Blackie came up from behind and sidled between James and Mandy.

Mandy stared at James. 'What set the birds off if it wasn't Blackie after all?'

'Search me!' James looked all round the huge garden for the culprits, but saw nothing.

The pheasants made a great din as they flew off. A door in the house flew open and Mr Western strode out. 'Foxes!' he cried. 'Dennis, a couple of foxes are after the pheasants!' He called his farm manager out of the house after him. 'Pests! Vermin! Let's get after them as quick as we can!'

By this time, James had tight hold of Blackie's collar. He didn't want him getting in the line of fire as the two men came out with their shotguns.

'How do they know it's foxes?' Mandy breathed. She crouched beside James and Blackie in the shelter of the hedge, watching the heavy birds fly overhead.

'Look!' James had seen them at last.

Two foxes swerved across the lawn towards them. Ears pricked, amber eyes gleaming, they ran silently and swiftly across the frost-covered grass.

'*That* was the trail we saw!' James whispered. 'Not Blackie!'

'Shh!' Mandy longed for the foxes to reach the safety of the hedge before Mr Western and Dennis Saville spotted them. She wouldn't want to see any creature harmed by a gun. And the two foxes were beautiful. Their coats were red and silky smooth. Their chests and bellies were white, their ears and legs were black. They carried their magnificent bushy tails low to the ground. But it was their eyes, a bright, shining amber, edged with black, which fascinated Mandy. The foxes ran side by side, deprived of their prey, for by now the birds were long gone.

Blackie gave a deep, rumbling growl. James held tight. 'I think they'll make it!' he whispered.

The foxes had reached the edge of the lawn. Silent as shadows they came, slinking into the

hedge a few metres from where James, Mandy and Blackie hid.

'Over there!' Sam Western spotted the fresh tracks. He heard the movement of animals brushing against undergrowth, of twigs snapping underfoot. He raised his gun to his shoulder and aimed it at the hedge.

'Don't shoot!' Mandy stood up. It was time to show themselves. If they distracted the men's attention, the foxes would be able to slide off unnoticed. She felt James stand beside her, heard Blackie bark, then saw a red flash of fox out of the corner of her eye. The pair were off, through the hedge, up the open hillside towards the Beacon.

'What on earth . . . ?' Mr Western lowered his gun. 'Is that you, Mandy Hope?'

She stepped into view between the wide iron gates. 'Yes. We're collecting holly for our Christmas decorations.' Her voice held steady, though her legs trembled. It had been a close thing for the two foxes.

'Collecting holly?' He strode down the drive. 'Look here, you nearly got yourselves shot. We're after a couple of foxes. Did you see them? Which way did they go? Flinging open the gate, Sam Western waited for Mandy's reply.

Mandy swallowed hard. With a warning glance at James, she waved her arm towards the valley. 'I think they headed that way.'

She sent the two men hurrying off in the wrong direction, boots crunching over the frost, breathing clouds of steam into the cold, crisp air.

'Oh, Mr Hope, whatever is wrong with poor Toby?' Mrs Ponsonby sailed into the crowded waiting-room at Animal Ark, her mongrel dog tucked under her arm. Her broad face was red and she was out of breath as she pushed past other patients waiting quietly in the queue. 'Excuse me, but this is an emergency. Poor Toby can hardly breathe. He needs to see a vet immediately!'

Adam Hope came out from behind the reception desk and guided her straight into a treatment room. He beckoned Mandy to follow. 'Jean, could you put my appointments back by ten minutes, please?' he called to the receptionist, who began to fend off the grumbles and complaints of the other pet owners in the waiting-room.

Mandy went in and closed the door after them. She watched her dad begin to examine the dog.

'He's certainly breathing heavily. He hasn't been

left in a room that's much too warm, without any ventilation, by any chance?' Mr Hope placed his stethoscope on Toby's chest.

'Of course not. Oh, it's a heart attack, isn't it? How dreadful. Is it the excitement of Christmas, Mr Hope? Toby loves Christmas, but he does tend to get over-excited. Oh dear, it is; it's his heart. I knew it!'

Toby stood on the treatment table panting heavily.

'No, I don't think so, Mrs Ponsonby. Toby's heart sounds fine. Now, there's no discharge from the eyes or the nose, as far as I can tell.'

Mrs Ponsonby still feared the worst. 'Oh, it's distemper, isn't it?'

Mandy's dad shook his head.

'Pneumonia, then?'

'No, his lungs are fine too.' Mr Hope stood back to scratch his chin. 'How long has Toby been like this?'

'Ten whole minutes! I popped into the post office to see Mrs McFarlane. I left my precious Toby and Pandora outside, and when I came out, there he was, in this terrible state. I was convinced he was about to breathe his last, so I rushed him straight here in the car.'

'Hmm. Well he seems to be improving now.'

Mandy agreed. The scruffy mongrel was already wagging his tail. His little black nose was moist, his eyes bright. Certainly there didn't seem to be much wrong with him now.

'Tell me, Mrs Ponsonby, was there anybody else around when you came out of the post office? Anyone with a dog, for instance?'

The large, fussy woman paused to consider. 'So you think Toby might have caught something infectious from another dog? Well, let's see now. Yes, the new people from the Old Vicarage were close by. Mr and Mrs Dixon, isn't it? And they had their brute with them. Of course, that must be it!' She bristled and shook with outrage at the idea.

'Their brute?' Mr Hope was puzzled.

'A rough collie,' Mandy explained. She knew the Dixon family had moved into the large old house with their dog and her litter of five pups.

'Great big nasty woolly thing. All that shaggy fur; so unhygienic. No wonder Toby's caught something unpleasant!'

'Maybe, maybe not!'

Mandy saw the flicker of a smile at the corners of her father's mouth.

'Is this dog a bitch?' he asked.

'To be sure. Henrietta. Such a silly name for a rough brute like that. Yes, a female.'

'Hmm.'

Mandy could see from her father's hesitation that he didn't know how to break the news. She felt her own mouth begin to quiver.

'Well, er, Mrs Ponsonby, I don't think there's anything seriously the matter with Toby. Look, you can see he's already beginning to calm down nicely.'

'Nothing the matter? But this is an emergency!'

'No, luckily, you were mistaken.' He glanced at Mandy and took a deep breath. 'The fact is, Mrs Ponsonby, Toby was just a little overexcited, shall we say. Let's put it down to the fact that he must have fallen prey to the lovely Henrietta's charms.'

Mandy put one hand to her mouth and coughed. In a flurry of sudden activity, she began to tidy a shelf in a corner of the room.

'Fallen prey . . . ?' Mrs Ponsonby blushed bright red to the roots of her blue-rinsed hair. 'Oh, I see. You mean he was attracted to a member of the opposite sex? Oh my! Oh dear.' She frowned and tutted, then hurried forward to scoop Toby into her arms. 'You're sure, now, Mr Hope? You don't think we need a second opinion from Mrs Hope?'

Mandy's mum was hard at work in the treatment room next door. Mandy had shown Ernie Bell in there with his young cat, Tiddles.

'Quite sure.' Adam Hope was firm. 'I think you should take Toby home, give him a nice cool drink and let him have a nap. He'll be right as rain after that, you'll see.'

'Yes, I'm sure you're right. Come along, Toby.' Mrs Ponsonby couldn't leave fast enough. 'It's so good of you to see us so promptly, Adam. But now we mustn't take up any more of your valuable time!'

Mandy watched her rush out in a wave of sweet perfume. 'Whoo-oo, *Adam*!' she teased her dad.

But already Jean, the receptionist, was showing the next patient in, and they soon forgot about Mrs Ponsonby and lovelorn Toby. There was a spaniel with a swollen earflap, and a budgie who was going bald. Then there was a litter of kittens for Mandy to feed and clean in the residential unit, and a dozen other jobs to keep her busy until teatime. After tea, she was hoping to go with her mother to the Old Vicarage, where, with a bit of luck, she would meet the gorgeous Henrietta!

Two

'Hi, Mandy, need any help putting up the decorations?'

At four o'clock James popped in to see her. He'd taken Blackie home after their adventure at Upper Welford Hall, but now he was back. The waiting-room was emptying out, and Mandy was busy tying bunches of holly together with string, ready to hang over the doors.

'Hi, James. Yes, great.' After the holly, they could hang silver streamers. She explained her ideas and they set to to make the room look as Christmassy as possible.

'You don't think you're going a wee bit over the

top?' Jean asked, as James and Mandy pinned the streamers from corner to corner and hung holly from every shelf and cornice. She ticked off the last patients and got ready to leave.

'Why not? Isn't that what Christmas is all about?' Simon, the Animal Ark nurse, came out of a treatment room and nodded his approval. 'It looks great!'

'Thanks.' James climbed down from a stool and stood back to admire their efforts.

'Will you be going to the grand ceremony on Friday?' Simon asked Jean. 'You know, the big occasion!'

The receptionist sniffed. 'I'm not sure. I think I'd rather have our usual carol service outside the Fox and Goose.'

'Oh come on, Jean, it'll make a nice change.' Simon was young and ready to move with the times. 'How often do we get the chance to see a famous soap star in the flesh?'

Mandy pricked up her ears. 'What famous soap star?' This was the first she'd heard of it. Normally at Christmas, everyone in Welford got together to sing and have a party in the village hall.

'You know, Joe Wortley from *Dale End*. He's

coming to turn on the Christmas lights. Hadn't you heard?'

'Not *the* Joe Wortley?' Mandy's eyes lit up. She watched the popular television series whenever she could. Joe Wortley played the young, good-looking doctor, Justin Scott.

From behind her desk Jean tutted. 'What's wrong with good old Father Christmas? Some of us prefer the tried and tested ways, Simon. Ask any of the old-timers around here.'

But Mandy was getting carried away. 'It sounds great! Whose idea was it?' She rolled up the ball of string and put the scissors back behind the desk.

'The Dixons, I think. They're personal friends of Joe Wortley and they invited him to Welford for Christmas. They asked him to turn on the lights as a special favour. He isn't even going to charge for appearing.'

'I'll be there!' James too was excited. 'What time does it begin?'

'Seven-thirty, outside the pub.' Simon turned back to Jean. 'There'll be carols as well, you know. Why don't you come?'

'I might.'

'Come on. Just because the Dixons are new to

the village isn't a good reason to snub them. They didn't intend to upset anyone.'

'No, but they should have consulted with the Christmas committee first.' Jean was a member of the committee, along with Ernie Bell, Mrs Ponsonby and Mandy's gran. 'I call it very high-handed.'

'Well, maybe. But staying away isn't the answer. Everyone else is going to be there, you know.'

It would be a hard job to convince Jean, Mandy realised. For herself, she was too thrilled about Joe Wortley to take much notice. 'He's my favourite actor in the whole series!' she told James. 'And, just think, he's going to be in Welford this coming Friday!'

'. . . All that fuss,' Jean grumbled quietly in the background. 'Just think of the money that's been spent on those lights!'

'I'm going to get his autograph!' James vowed.

'Me too!' Mandy could hardly wait.

'. . . The Dixons, the Parker Smythes; these wealthy families, they're all the same . . .' Jean sighed.

'Maybe he'll bring some other actors from *Dale End* with him too!' Mandy pictured a whole host of television stars.

'. . . More money than sense,' Jean said, snapping the appointment book closed and buttoning up her coat.

Mandy was still bubbling with excitement when she drove with her mum and James into the village after surgery had ended.

'Did I tell you we saw two foxes up near the Beacon?' she asked Emily Hope, as they swept past the post office. The village streetlamps glowed, and all the houses were lit up as people arrived home from work.

'Three times,' Mrs Hope reminded her with a smile. 'And in broad daylight too. That's unusual. They're pretty secretive creatures as a rule.'

'Why don't farmers like them?' James asked. They hadn't told anyone about Mr Western's hasty call for his gun as soon as he'd spotted the intruders on his lawn. Mandy and he thought it best not to mention how close they'd come to peering down the wrong end of the barrel. 'I mean, I know they're supposed to kill chickens. But it's up to the farmers to make sure their hens are safely locked up at night, isn't it?'

'It depends how you look at it.' Emily Hope drove through the village to drop James off before she and Mandy doubled back to call in on vets' business at the Old Vicarage. 'Like most things. Some people see foxes as pests because they seem to kill without reason. Even if they're not hungry, they'll slaughter a whole coop full of chickens. They even say a fox will kill a young lamb, though I've never seen that myself.'

'I think they just blame foxes because they have to blame someone.' Mandy sprang to the animals' defence. 'They call them cunning, but that just means clever, really. They're cleverer than a lot of people, come to that!'

'Maybe.' The car pulled up at James's gate and Mrs Hope let him out. 'As a matter of fact, foxes aren't such a serious threat to farmers. They mostly hunt voles and other small mammals. They eat fruit and beetles, grass, cereals; anything they can get hold of. They're especially partial to earthworms, actually!'

'And the contents of our dustbin!' James added. 'My mum keeps saying we've got foxes in our garden.'

'She's probably right. There are a lot of urban foxes around now. It's easier for them to find food in towns and villages than in the open countryside.'

'I wish we had them in *our* garden,' Mandy said. 'I'd love to see them out of my bedroom window first thing in the morning!'

'Try putting out a plateful of worms then!' James grinned and said goodbye. 'Good luck at the vicarage.'

Mandy and Mrs Hope were going to meet the Dixons for the first time. Mrs Dixon had called Animal Ark and arranged a call-out visit. She said that the five collie pups needed their second round of vaccinations. So Mandy and her mum said goodbye to James and drove back to the centre of the village.

The Old Vicarage stood out of sight behind the church in big grounds that rolled down to the river's edge. The house was enormous. It was built of stone, with strong pillars at the top of a flight of wide steps leading up to the main door. Inside, Mandy glimpsed bright chandeliers, polished floors and dark red patterned carpets. She followed her mother, smoothing her blonde hair and tugging at the hem of her jumper. Somehow, a house like this made her nervous.

A girl of about her own age answered the door. She was tall and skinny, with jet-black hair worn in a straight fringe and falling like curtains on either side of her pale face. Her eyes were light grey, her mouth unsmiling.

'Hello, we've come to give the puppies their injections,' Mrs Hope said pleasantly, introducing herself and Mandy.

The girl sniffed and led them across the hall. 'Mummy!' she yelled up the curving staircase. 'It's the vet!' Then she disappeared into a room where music blared and a television screen flickered.

A woman came down to greet them. 'I'm Helena Dixon. You must be Emily Hope. The pups are in the utility room at the back of the house. It's quite warm in there, and it means they're out of the way, not getting under everyone's feet, you know.' She smiled and bustled ahead. Like her daughter, she was slim and dark. She wore red lipstick and gold earrings, and her nails were painted the same shade of red as her lips, Mandy noticed.

'You say the pups are twelve weeks old?' Emily Hope followed quietly. 'And they had their first round of injections before you came to Welford?'

'That's right. The little rascals; I'd no idea rough collie pups got into so much mischief. That's why we keep them out there, otherwise our poor furniture wouldn't be fit to be seen.'

Mrs Dixon took them through the kitchen and out into a bare room lined with a washing-machine, dryer and freezer. 'Of course, it's different with Henrietta. She was fully house-trained when we got her. She's in with Sophie watching *Dale End* on TV. But as for the pups, the sooner they go off to good homes the better!' she exclaimed as she switched on the light.

'Oh!' Mandy couldn't stop herself from crying out in delight as five little furry bundles hurtled towards them. They were a mixture of black, brown and white; tiny, shaggy miniatures, some with black patches over one eye, some with white paws, some with brown paws, and all with shiny button-noses and pink tongues that lolled and panted as they leaped and tumbled to the floor.

'You see what I mean?' Helena Dixon stepped back out of their way. 'I can't wear a decent pair of trousers with these puppies jumping up all the time.'

Mrs Hope put her bag on the floor and took off her jacket. 'OK, now I'm going to give them each a jab for distemper, hepatitis and parvovirus. You haven't found a problem with any of the pups so far?'

Mrs Dixon frowned, then shrugged.

'I mean, are they all fit and healthy? They're all equally active?'

'Much too active, if you ask me.'

Emily Hope asked Mandy to hold the first pup as she prepared a syringe. 'They certainly look lively enough.'

The four other little bundles of fur skidded and flung themselves at Mandy and Emily Hope. One in particular charged without looking where he was going. He crashed into a chair leg and rolled over.

'That's Nipper,' Mrs Dixon said with a sigh. 'So called because he nips about all over the place. And that one you're holding is Flora. That's Daisy, that's Henry and that's Olivia.' She named them each in turn. Flora yelped as Mrs Hope gave her the jab. Mandy stroked her, then let her go.

'Number two!' Out came the second syringe. Mrs Hope asked Mandy to move on to Daisy. 'You're making sure to worm them?' she said to Helena Dixon.

'My daughter, Sophie, does that. You met her when you arrived. But yes, I'm quite sure that side is taken care of.' The puppies' owner sidestepped another frantic charge. 'Listen, you don't mind if I leave you to it, do you? We have a guest arriving for dinner.' She began to back out of the utility room into the kitchen.

'No, of course not. Mandy and I can manage here.' Emily Hope smiled and carried on with her work. 'We'll see ourselves out.'

Obviously glad to escape, Helena Dixon closed the door behind her.

Only then did Mandy relax. She played with the pups while her mum checked their paws, their ears, their eyes and throats. Mandy tickled them and rubbed their tummies, made them squirm and wriggle with pleasure. Henry jumped into her lap as she sat cross-legged on the tiled floor, Olivia yelped to be picked up. Daisy and Flora rolled on their backs and waved their legs in the air, while Nipper charged and bumped straight into Mrs Hope's bag.

'Oops!' Mandy laughed as her mum set him back on his feet. Nipper shook himself and charged on.

'Come on, we're all finished here.' Mrs Hope watched his wobbly course. 'Time to go!'

Reluctantly, Mandy stood up and made sure that the pups were all safely inside the room, then she followed her mum quickly to the door and turned out the light. Together they slipped out of the kitchen, leaving behind the sound of high yelps and little paws scrabbling on the bare floor in the dark utility room.

Out in the hall, Mandy noticed the television still on in the room where Sophie had been. The door stood ajar, but there was no sign of Henrietta or of Sophie herself. *At least she could have shown some interest in the puppies*, Mandy thought.

She didn't like what she'd seen so far of the newcomers to the village. For all their money and their famous friend, neither Sophie nor her mother had struck her as particularly happy. In fact, they seemed cool and stand-offish.

And anyone who can lock puppies up in a boring, bare utility room doesn't deserve to keep them! Mandy thought.

She headed across the richly-patterned rug in the hallway, grumbling to herself, following her mother towards the big main door.

Suddenly, the doorbell rang and stopped them in their tracks. The television went off and Sophie shot out into the hall. Mrs Dixon came running downstairs, newly-changed into a tight black dress and high-heeled shoes. Her husband strode out of yet another room. They all made for the door at once.

Mandy and Emily Hope stepped quickly aside

as Sophie reached the door first. She pulled it open, and in stepped . . . yes! Mandy's mouth fell open. She managed to clamp it shut again just in time . . . In stepped Joe Wortley himself!

'Joe, darling, how nice to see you!' Helena Dixon drew him into the warm house.

The actor kissed and embraced the two female Dixons and shook hands with Mr Dixon. He was just how he looked on television; the same handsome face with its square jaw and grey eyes, the fair hair. *But he's not as tall as he looks on telly*, Mandy thought with a tiny glimmer of disappointment.

'Come in, come in.' Mr Dixon was all smiles. 'We're glad you could make it.'

'I came straight here from filming in Walton,' Joe said. He flashed an absent-minded smile in the direction of Mandy and her mum.

His voice was as deep and kind as it was when he played Dr Justin Scott, Mandy thought. It struck her that she was actually in the same room as Joe Wortley and she felt her heart begin to race. He did look a bit older in real life. She studied the wrinkles at the corners of his eyes, the sagging flesh under his chin. Still, she tried not to mind.

'Come on, Mandy.' Emily Hope was trying to

slide out of the door. She succeeded in pulling Mandy after her.

'Who was that?' they heard the great man say, as Sophie closed the door after them.

'Only the vet,' Helena Dixon explained. 'Oh, Joe, you haven't seen our gorgeous little rough collie pups, have you? You must come and look at them now, right this minute, before we do anything else! Wait and see, they're absolutely adorable . . . !'

Mandy floated down the steps. Her feet crunched on the gravel drive. She waited under the starlit sky as her mum unlocked the car door. *Joe Wortley! Just wait until I tell everyone I've actually seen him in real life!*

'Hop in, Mandy. Are you OK?' Emily Hope started the engine.

She nodded. 'Isn't he . . . wonderful, Mum?' She couldn't think of any other word to describe him.

'Hmm, I suppose so, if you like that sort of thing.' They rode off out of the grounds, past the church, back into the village. The lights of the Fox and Goose glowed warmly. The pub was busy, the carpark crowded.

Mandy made out the outline of a tall Christmas tree and strings of lights decorating the yard and the pub itself; all waiting to be turned on by Joe Wortley this coming Friday. 'Didn't you like him?' she breathed, turning to her mum.

'What? Yes, I expect he's very charming.' Emily Hope's mind was on something else as she turned into the lane leading to Animal Ark.

'What are you thinking about?' Mandy wondered if it had something to do with the Dixons' puppies; something that her mum hadn't mentioned when they were in the house. 'There's nothing wrong, is there?'

'No, no, I'm probably worrying about nothing.'

Animal Ark was in sight; the familiar wooden sign, the cosy old house and the surgery at the back. 'Sure?' If there was a problem, Mandy would rather know.

'Yes, I was just thinking about little Nipper. I wonder why he doesn't look where he's going. But it's probably just that he's got too much energy, like most puppies of his age. It's nothing. Come on, let's go and see what your dad's been up to while we've been out!'

Three

'. . . Putting up the Christmas tree, that's what I've been up to!' Adam Hope cried. 'And now I'm covered from head to toe in pine needles.'

Mandy brushed him down. 'Can we decorate it straight away?' she asked. Once the tree was up in the big cottage kitchen, it really felt like Christmas.

So they called Gran and Grandad Hope over from Lilac Cottage, and together the whole family hung silver baubles, ribbons and lights on the tree.

'More tea?' Gran was in charge of the teapot. She came round with refills, and a plate of hot mince-pies.

'Please.' Adam Hope stood on a stool, trying to

perch the fairy on the top of the tree.

'Yes, please.' Mandy's grandad plugged in the lights. 'Hey presto!' he said as he turned on the switch. The lights winked prettily.

'Ooh, yes, I'd love another cup!' Mrs Hope carried presents to put under the tree. They were shiny and bright; big boxes, small squashy parcels, round things and long, thin, mysterious things.

Mandy was trying to guess what each present might be when the phone rang. 'I'll get it!' She raced to answer.

'Hello, Mandy?'

She recognised the throaty voice. 'Yes, hello, Mrs Ponsonby.' She rolled her eyes at her mum and dad.

'Say we're busy!' Adam Hope whispered, almost tottering from his stool at the sound of the name.

'Listen, my dear, I know your mother and dear Adam must be terribly busy . . .'

'Yes, actually, they are.' Mandy pulled another face. 'It's not Toby, is it?'

'Toby? Oh no, dear, he's quite recovered, thank you. No, what I was wondering was could you possibly pass on a message? It's about foxes.'

Mandy grew more interested. 'Have you seen some at Bleakfell Hall?' She wondered if the pair from Upper Welford had made their way down into the valley after all.

'Not seen, exactly. But I have definite evidence that there are foxes in my garden. I got back home this evening to find that my dustbins had been ransacked. The lids were off and there were tins and waste paper strewn all over the stable yard. Absolutely no doubt in my mind that foxes were responsible. And that makes me rather worried about my poor Pandora and Toby. I mean to say, foxes are such vicious creatures. What would happen if brave little Toby were to try and chase them? He could be terribly injured.'

'Oh, I don't think a fox would – ' Mandy got no further with her sentence.

'I've been speaking to Sam Western about the problem, and he agrees with me. We feel we should record all our sightings and find out their preferred spots. Then, when we've established a pattern of their movements, it will be much easier to track them down and drive them out.'

Mandy clenched her teeth and kept silent. She knew there was no point in arguing with Mrs Ponsonby once she got a bee in her bonnet.

'I volunteered to organise things. I call it our Fox Watch scheme. We need to find out how many foxes there are prowling round our gardens at night, and to warn people to keep their pets indoors, just in case. I promised to tell everyone in the village, so that we could set up an early-warning chain of phone calls whenever anyone sights one of these pests. And that's the message I'd like you to pass on to your parents, Mandy, dear. If anyone at Animal Ark happens across any sign of a fox, please telephone me and let me know immediately!'

Mandy stuttered out a promise. 'Fox Watch!' she cried as soon as she put down the phone. 'Mrs Ponsonby can't know for sure that it was foxes who upset her bins. She wasn't even there!'

Gran listened and calmed her down. 'Now you know what Mrs Ponsonby is like. She is prone to exaggerate. I'm sure other people in Welford will take a more sensible view of the foxes. "Live and let live" is the motto.'

'Yes, and anyway, it's nearly Christmas,' Grandad added. 'The spirit of goodwill should reach Mrs Ponsonby eventually. In other words, she'll probably get over this fox business sooner than you think. I wouldn't worry about it if I were you.'

So Mandy let herself think that it was all a storm in a teacup. She listened to the grown-ups planning a carol-singing group to go round and visit all the houses in the neighbourhood the following night.

'If we can't have our usual Christmas Eve carol concert outside the Fox and Goose because of this big TV star ceremony, we'll just have to fix up an alternative,' Gran said. 'We'll wrap up warm in our hats and scarves and go round singing all the old favourites.'

> '*Good King Wenceslas looked out,*
> *On the Feast of Stee-phen!*'

Adam Hope piped up.

'We'll collect money for a children's hospital charity. Would you and James like to come?' Gran asked.

> '*When the snow lay round about,*
> *Deep and crisp and ee-ven!*'

'You bet!' Mandy was back in a good mood. Now it really was almost Christmas!

> '*Christmas is coming,*
> *The goose is getting fat . . .*'

Mr Hope strode up the drive to Upper Welford Hall. He rang on the doorbell.

> '*Please put a penny*
> *In the old man's hat!*'

Sam Western opened the door. He frowned at the band of carol singers, led by Adam Hope. Behind him was a group of a dozen or more, hats pulled well down, song sheets fluttering in the stiff breeze. Mandy and her grandparents were among them, though her mum had had to stay on call at Animal Ark. Mrs Ponsonby had insisted on coming. And there was James and another friend, Susan Collins, as well as Ernie Bell and his old pal, Walter Pickard. The two old men growled and grunted their way through the songs, stamping their feet and looking forward to a nice warm fire and a drink back at the Fox and Goose.

Mr Hope rattled the collecting-box. 'All in a good cause,' he said cheerfully.

The landowner dug into his trouser pocket, then demanded another song for his money. The singers struck up with 'The Twelve Days of Christmas'. Mandy could hear Mrs Ponsonby belting out the words at the top of her voice.

'Thank you, thank you, and Happy Christmas!' Sam Western cried when they reached the fifth day.

> '*On the fifth day of Christ-mas*
> *My true love sent to me . . .*
> *Five go-old rings!*'

'Whoa, thank you. I'll catch my death of cold out here!' Briskly he stepped back and closed the door.

Then there was much scuffling and nudging as the band turned and made off down the drive, torches raking across the perfect lawns, feet crunching on the frosty gravel. At the gate, Gran took charge and headed them all off to High Cross.

'Lydia will give us a better welcome than we got here,' she promised. 'So come on, raise your voices one more time!'

Mandy and James hung back as the others went ahead to Lydia Fawcett's old-fashioned farm. Their throats were dry, their fingers tingling with cold.

'That's where the foxes headed off to, remember?' James said quietly. He pointed towards the stone cross on the hill, known locally as the Beacon. It was a landmark for miles around.

Mandy shone her torch up the hill, listening to

the new song. 'We shouldn't stay too long,' she warned. 'They'll think we've got lost.'

James took no notice. 'Maybe the foxes are still around.' He left the track and stepped on to the rough heather. 'If we're lucky, we might see them.'

'If they are, I'm definitely not letting Mrs Ponsonby know!' Mandy was still worked up about last night's phone call. She told James about the Fox Watch scheme, and the cruel plan to drive the foxes out of the village.

'Shh, hang on!' James caught her arm. 'Switch your torch off, Mandy. Look up there: it's them!'

Instinct made her crouch low amongst the frozen heather beside James. She looked up the slope, towards a clump of hawthorn trees, feeling the silence gather. There on the brow of the hill, she saw the foxes.

They were dark shadows in the moonlight. But as Mandy's eyes grew used to the dark, she could pick out more detail. 'You're right, it's the same ones!'

'Shh!'

'What are they doing?' The foxes were rolling on the ground near the trees, then jumping up and chasing their own tails.

'Playing,' James whispered.

'At this time of night?' Mandy crept closer and spotted a movement in one of the trees. 'Look, James, there's an owl up there on that low branch!'

The big, pale bird sat staring at the foxes, chest feathers puffed out, eyes unblinking.

As the foxes whirled in tight circles, still chasing their tails, they steered nearer and nearer to the hypnotised owl.

'He'd better watch out!' Mandy whispered. The foxes were almost within reach of the bird. They pretended to ignore the owl, but Mandy could see what they were up to. Once they were close enough, the foxes would leave off playing and pounce.

Round and round they went, somersaulting and bucking, as if they'd taken leave of their senses. The unwary owl was fascinated.

Then, as they raced around the tree-trunk, directly underneath the owl, one fox leaped up at the branch with snapping jaws.

Crack! Mandy and James heard the sharp teeth snap shut. The owl flapped its wings and rose from the branch just in time. The fox fell back to the ground, disappointed.

'Phew.' James breathed again. 'I've never seen anything like that before!'

'Amazing.' Mandy backed off as the foxes sniffed round the trunk then sloped off, still hungry.

'They were trying to fool the owl into thinking they hadn't seen him!' James watched the two dog-like animals melt into the shadows of the trees.

Now that the foxes had gone, Mandy wanted to hurry and join the others. They jogged down the track to High Cross Farm and arrived just in time to sing the last song for Lydia. Miss Fawcett stood at her door, arms folded, smiling and humming along. At the end of the song, she invited the whole crowd inside for a drink.

'What were you two up to out there?' she asked James as she gave him a mug of cocoa. 'I noticed you creeping up when it was nearly all over. You didn't nip into the barn to say hello to my goats by any chance?'

'No. We were up by the Beacon. We saw two foxes!' he told her.

'But don't tell anyone!' Mandy broke in. 'Mrs Ponsonby thinks they should be driven out.'

'Ah yes, I heard.' Lydia Fawcett smiled gently. 'Fox Watch, isn't it? Don't worry, I won't let on.'

'Thanks.' Mandy knew the secret was safe with Lydia. Though she was a farmer, she held unusual views about wild animals like rabbits and foxes, refusing to let others shoot them on her property. 'These foxes were doing something strange. They tried to fool an owl into thinking they hadn't seen him, and they managed to get close enough to grab him.'

'Almost,' James nodded. 'But not quite.'

Lydia smiled again. 'Sly old things. Were they running rings round him?'

Mandy nodded. 'Chasing their own tails. It was like they hypnotised the owl.'

'That's exactly what they did. Foxes are well known for it.' Lydia confirmed what James and Mandy had just seen. 'They're very clever animals. It's what people mean when they say foxes can charm the birds out of the trees!'

The carol singers left High Cross Farm and trooped down the hill into the village, calling at houses on the way. The collecting-box was heavy and jangling with coins, and their voices hoarse, as at last they turned down by the side of the church for a final call at the Old Vicarage.

' "While Shepherds Watched"!' Mandy's gran suggested, with a stern eye on Mandy and James. 'And no fooling around with the words this time!'

The singers gathered at the bottom of the steps and struck up the first verse.

   '*While shepherds washed their socks by night,*'

Mandy sang;

      '*All seated on the ground . . .*'

'Mandy!' Adam Hope warned out of the corner of his mouth.

She grinned up at him. But just on the burst of the next line of the carol she saw her mum's car pull up in the drive. She turned and ran to meet her.

'Hi, Mandy. How did you all get on?'

'Fantastic. We saw the foxes trying to charm an owl!'

Mrs Hope put an arm round her shoulder and walked towards the door. 'I meant the carol singing.'

'Great. But what are you doing here?'

'Oh, I was on my way home from another call and I just thought I would pop in and take a second look at the Dixons' pups before they send them all off to nice new homes.'

'Can I come, please?' Mandy never missed a

chance to help her mum and dad. She saw the door open in answer to the carol singers, and Mrs Dixon appear with a handful of loose change.

'Sure. Stand to one side while the thirsty hordes head for the Fox and Goose.' Mrs Hope waited for the carol singers to disperse. 'Mandy's coming with me. We won't be long,' she told Adam. They arranged to meet up with him and Gran and Grandad Hope at Lilac Cottage. James had already been met by his own dad, and soon there was no one except Mandy and her mum left in the drive.

'Come on,' Helena Dixon said. She had her fingers hitched through the collar of a fully grown rough collie, who wagged her tail furiously and gazed at her with intelligent eyes.

'This must be Henrietta.' Mrs Hope stooped to pat the dog as she went in.

The gorgeous Henrietta! Mandy smiled to herself. The dog certainly was beautiful. Her dark eyes were big and wide, her sharp ears were pricked above her fine, long face. And she was an all-over bundle of energy and fun, just like her pups.

'You said on the phone that you wanted to check the puppies,' Mrs Dixon said with a frown, leading them through to the back of the house. 'I take it there's nothing wrong?'

'Well, I'm not certain, so I thought I'd better come back and see. I've been reading up about a condition which is quite common in this breed.' Mandy's mum sounded businesslike.

Suddenly alert, Mandy followed. The pups were being kept in the utility room, as before. They barked and bounced with joy when the light went on and they saw their visitors.

'I do hope there isn't a problem,' Mrs Dixon said with a sigh. 'We've already found homes for three of the pups. I wouldn't want anything to go wrong now.'

'Well, let's see.' Emily Hope decided to begin with Henrietta herself. She took a strong light from her pocket and shone it directly into the dog's eyes.

Mandy watched. Why did her mum want to examine the mother as well?

'There's an inherited weakness in collies,' she explained. 'It's called collie eye, but to be more exact, it's CEA, or collie eye anomaly.' Next she picked up one of the puppies and shone the light into his eyes.

'Meaning what?' This was bad news as far as Mrs Dixon was concerned. They heard irritation in her voice.

'It's a disease of the retina inside the eye. The

retina can become detached, and then of course the dog will go blind. There's some level of CEA present in a high percentage of collies, unfortunately.' Mrs Hope moved on through the second and third puppies, examining their eyes under the strong beam of the torch.

'Here's Flora.' Mrs Dixon handed her the fourth puppy.

'Fine,' Mandy's mum said. 'Now, Nipper, let's take a look at you.' She took the last pup from Mandy. He squirmed and wriggled, trying to lick their hands.

When she stood up she was frowning.

'Well?' Helena Dixon wanted the verdict.

'Firstly, I'm pretty sure Henrietta does have some level of CEA. As far as I can tell from a quick examination, she only has partial sight in her left eye. Now, it's not severe enough to be a big problem for her, thank goodness, and of course she can make up for sight loss through her hearing and sense of smell.' Emily Hope gave a full, calm explanation.

'What about the puppies?' Mandy realised that Henrietta might have passed the condition on to them. She felt her stomach curl into a tight knot as she held on to Nipper and stroked his soft head.

'Flora, Daisy, Olivia and Henry are clear.' Emily Hope slipped both hands into her pockets and studied the fifth puppy. 'But it was Nipper I was concerned about. He didn't seem to have a good sense of direction when we first saw him, and you remember he kept tripping over things?'

Mandy nodded. Her hands began to tremble.

'That's what made me come back. And I'm afraid I was right about him. Nipper does have quite a high level of CEA in both eyes.'

'You mean he's blind?' Mrs Dixon tried to grasp the full picture.

Mandy hugged him to her.

'No, not completely. But his vision is very restricted. The problem is, collie eye can lead to the retina becoming completely detached in future years. And then of course, the dog would become blind.'

Nipper's pink tongue rasped along Mandy's knuckles as he begged for her to stroke him again.

'And what do you suggest we do?'

The four healthy puppies skidded along the tiles, playing and yelping, while Henrietta sidled up alongside Mandy and Nipper.

'Of course, the decision is up to you. Some owners are prepared to keep a dog with poor eyesight. It takes a lot of extra patience and care, but it can be very rewarding. All these dogs are extremely friendly and loyal, and you would find the same thing even in one with a disability. On the other hand, breeders are keen to screen out the gene responsible for CEA, so they might suggest putting the puppy down.'

There was a horrible pause. Mandy swallowed hard and waited for Mrs Dixon to reply. Her hand shook as she stroked Nipper's head.

'Would it be difficult for us to find an owner for him?'

'Possibly. But he's an affectionate little chap. Maybe someone will be willing to take him.'

'Oh, I don't know. No one has chosen him so far; perhaps because he's obviously so much of a handful. And now we know why,' Mrs Dixon sighed. 'Perhaps it would be kinder . . .'

She didn't speak the words, but Mandy knew full well what she meant. *Perhaps it would be kinder to have Nipper put to sleep!*

'Take your time. Don't decide straight away,' Mrs Hope suggested.

'Yes, you're right. I'll talk to my husband.' Helena Dixon began to show them out. She took Nipper from Mandy and carried him with her through the house to the front door. 'Can we give you a ring when . . . if . . . you know . . . ?'

'Of course.' Mrs Hope said she was sorry about the news. 'I wish I could have given them all a clean bill of health,' she sighed. 'But do ring me at Animal Ark as soon as you've talked it through.'

Mandy hardly knew what she was doing as she got into the car and they drove off. She was breathing shallowly and her whole body was tense.

But she knew she couldn't say anything. After all, her mum was just doing her job like a good vet should. They had no right to interfere with the Dixons' decision.

As they drove past the church, the moon lit up the clock face on the square tower and the golden weather vane glinted. It swung round in the wind.

Will they? Won't they? Would Helena Dixon decide that half blind, Nipper was too much of a nuisance after all? And would she have him quietly and gently put to sleep?

Four

With the death threat hanging over Nipper, the run-up to Christmas for Mandy grew bumpier still.

'Mrs Ponsonby!' Jean sounded a warning note as a car pulled up in the surgery carpark early next day. Adam and Emily Hope disappeared swiftly into the treatment rooms.

'Ah, Mandy, my dear!' The Terror of Welford strode in with a dog tucked under each arm.

Mandy hadn't reacted quickly enough to get out of her way.

'No, no, don't disturb your mother and father. I know what busy people they are! You and Jean will do just as well.' She deposited Pandora, her overweight Pekinese, and Toby on the floor and delved into her outsize handbag for a batch of yellow leaflets. 'Now, listen, the surgery is an ideal location to hand out our Fox Watch warning pamphlets. Here they are, hot off the press. I need you to give out one of these to every single person who comes in. Is that clear?'

Jean took the pile and Mandy glimpsed the contents over the receptionist's shoulder. 'BEWARE FOXES!' she read. 'Keep Your Eyes Peeled for Welford's New Menace, the Urban Fox! Report any sighting to Fox Watch Scheme Leader, Mrs A. Ponsonby, Welford 338725.'

Jean took off her glasses and shook her head. 'Is this really necessary? I mean, I always consider it rather a privilege myself whenever a fox ventures into my little garden.'

She spoke meekly, but Mandy could have hugged her for sticking up for the much-insulted fox.

'Hmph!' Mrs Ponsonby could see that Jean needed advice. 'My dear, it's people like you who make Fox Watch's task so much more difficult. You entice them into the village with your ill-judged saucers of milk and left-overs from the dinner table. And where does that leave us? We're overrun with the creatures before you can turn around!'

'But I haven't seen a fox in a long, long time.' Jean protested her innocence.

'Then you should come to Bleakfell Hall and see the damage they do in my stable yard.'

As Mrs Ponsonby spoke, Toby and Pandora scuttled behind the desk and riffled through Jean's rubbish bin. Mandy bent down to pet them so that Mrs Ponsonby didn't see her face turn red with irritation.

'This morning I went out and what did I find? Two dustbins turned upside down and all their contents turfed out! Chicken bones and bacon rind devoured. Orange peel chewed by sharp teeth. Quite disgraceful!'

Jean sighed. 'I'll have to ask Adam and Emily if it would be all right for you to leave your leaflets here.' She disappeared into a treatment room, leaving the door open.

'Tell them that Mr Western is standing by with a group of fellow farmers. As soon as we've acquired a sufficient number of sightings in the village, their intention is to pin down the foxes' earths and flush them out!'

Mandy stood up with a sharp intake of breath. 'But, Mrs Ponsonby, you know what that means, don't you? The farmers round here hate foxes.

They won't just drive them out of the village, they'll shoot them as well!'

'Nonsense, dear. It will be quite sufficient for Sam Western to use his knowledge of the creatures to chase them out of the neighbourhood. He can block up the entrances to their earths, do whatever's necessary. But he doesn't actually have to destroy them. Don't be so silly.'

Mandy opened her mouth to protest again, but her dad emerged before she could frame a sentence.

'Good morning, Mrs Ponsonby.'

Mrs Ponsonby gave him a dazzling smile. 'Good morning, Adam. Please call me Amelia!'

'Um – er – Amelia, I'm afraid we can't take these leaflets from you. We have a policy here at Animal Ark never to take advertisements from outside bodies, and that would apply to Fox Watch, I'm afraid.' He pushed the pile back across the desk, polite but firm.

Mandy wanted to cheer.

Mrs Ponsonby's face fell. 'But this is hardly an advertisement, Adam. After all, we're not trying to sell a product.'

'No, but Emily and I feel we have to hold very strictly to our rule,' he insisted. 'I'm sorry.'

Try as she might, Mrs Ponsonby couldn't get him to change his mind. In the end, she had to put the leaflets back inside her bag and go off to try at the post office and the village hall for spaces on the notice-boards to announce her scheme.

'Well done, Dad,' Mandy sighed. She watched Toby and Pandora jump into the back of Mrs Ponsonby's car and drive off. 'But I wish Mr Western and his men weren't on her side.' She pictured them getting together, driving the foxes into the corners, raising their guns and shooting.

Adam Hope winked. 'Don't worry, love. Your

average fox can outsmart Sam Western and Amelia Ponsonby any day!'

Surgery that morning was full of two topics only: Mrs Ponsonby's Fox Watch and the forthcoming appearance in Welford of the famous Joe Wortley.

'. . . A friend of the Dixons,' people said in awed tones.

'. . . Staying with them over Christmas.'

'. . . My sister, Wendy, saw him in a Land-rover Discovery with Helena Dixon!'

'. . . So handsome, just like he is on the telly!'

Mandy came and went, standing in on Reception for Jean when she popped out on her lunch break. When the phone rang, she had trouble hearing what the speaker said because of the excited gossip about Friday night's grand switch-on.

'Hello, this is Animal Ark surgery. Who's that, please?'

'This is Helena Dixon. May I leave a message for Emily Hope, please?'

It was the phone call Mandy had been dreading. She steeled herself to hear the Dixons' decision about Nipper. *Yes, go ahead.* With one hand over her ear to cut out the noise in the waiting-room, she held her breath.

'It's about the puppy with the eye disorder. We talked it through last night and decided that the best thing to do was to have him put down.'

Mandy felt her heart thud and miss a beat.

'Are you still there? It seemed for the best. I wanted to ring you earlier this morning and arrange for it to be done as quickly as possible. But now I'm afraid it's been taken out of our hands.'

'What do you mean?' Mandy gathered her wits after the shock.

'Well, we knew that Sophie wasn't happy with the thought of it. In fact, she was rather upset. She went to bed in a very strange mood. This morning when she got up, she asked if she could take Henrietta and the two remaining puppies for a walk. That was Nipper and Olivia. The other three had been taken off to their new homes before breakfast.'

It was hard to concentrate on Mrs Dixon's voice. Mandy thought of all the dreadful things that might have happened during the walk.

'Well, Sophie had her way and took the three dogs out. I knew something was wrong when first Henrietta and then Olivia came back to the vicarage alone.'

'Why, what's happened to Sophie and Nipper?'

'That's the point. I was going frantic, about to call the police. Sophie had been gone for hours. I'd even been out to look for her myself. Then, when she did turn up at last, she was in a dreadful state. Her shoes were covered in mud and straw, and her new jacket was torn. She said that Nipper had run off and got lost, which is just like him, of course. The poor girl had hunted everywhere, but in the end she just had to come home without him.'

'You mean, Nipper is still lost?' Mandy gripped the phone, trying to piece together the full picture.'

'Exactly. Goodness knows where he went. But at least it does solve one problem.'

'What do you mean?'

'Since he's got himself lost, we don't have to ask you to put him to sleep for us. In fact, it's an impossibility. I thought it best to let you know.'

'He could freeze to death!' Mandy cycled to the Hunters' house as soon as she could. 'Poor little thing – the temperature drops way below freezing at night. James, what are we going to do?'

'We should go out and look for him.' James

settled his glasses firmly on to his nose and considered the problem. 'If it was any other lost animal, that's exactly what we'd do right now.'

'But the problem is, if we do find Nipper and take him back to the vicarage, the Dixons will only bring him to Animal Ark to be put down!' Mandy couldn't bear to think about it. 'They will, James. I'm absolutely sure!'

'But if we don't find him, he'll either starve or freeze.' James faced facts. 'Which would you rather?'

'Neither!' She paced up and down the Hunters' kitchen. 'He's out there somewhere, probably scared and in danger. We don't even know how well he can see with this eye disease. He could wander over the edge of a cliff up on the moor, or fall in the freezing river; anything!'

'We can't just leave him, can we?' James waited for Mandy to agree.

'No.' It was hard; one of the worst decisions she'd ever had to make. But when it came to it, it was better to have Nipper put to sleep by someone who cared.

'Let's go,' she whispered. Come on, before we change our minds.'

* * *

They rode out on their bikes and searched high and low for the lost puppy. They called in on the farms, from Greystones in the valley to High Cross on the hill, at the small terraced cottages in the main street, and the grand houses set back from the road. Everywhere the answer was the same.

'No, sorry, Mandy love, there's been no rough collie pup around here. But we'll ring Animal Ark if we do spot him.' Walter Pickard leaned on his garden gate and promised to help if he could.

'Poor little thing!' Marjorie and Joan Spry came to the door at The Riddings and cried out in unison. Their wrinkled, bird-like faces were full of concern. 'No, we certainly haven't seen him here, have we, Marjorie?'

'Unfortunately not, Joan. But we will look very hard and telephone you if we find him!'

Mandy and James thanked the elderly twins and went on from house to house.

The only person who didn't seem to care about Nipper was Mrs Ponsonby at Bleakfell Hall.

She was on her way out when they cycled up the drive. 'Tut-tut!' She shook her head. 'Trust the Dixons to lose a dog. Such a careless sort of family: that was my impression right from the start!' She locked her front door and waved goodbye to Toby and Pandora, who yapped through the window at her. 'Poor dears, they don't like being left in the house alone. But it would be dangerous to take them with me today!' she said darkly, raising her eyebrow in a sinister way.

'What do you mean?' Mandy let James scoot off to look round the big garden while she stayed with Mrs Ponsonby.

'Fox Watch!' The old lady mouthed the words. 'Shh! I don't want to worry Pandora!'

Alarmed, Mandy glanced round. 'Have you seen a fox?'

'No, not here. But I've just had a phone call from Dennis Saville up at the Hall to say that the foxes have been spotted. Mr Western has ordered him to round up the men to go and flush them out. Of course, as leader of the Fox Watch scheme, it's my duty to go and supervise arrangements! We're meeting in quarter of an hour.' She was in a hurry to be on her way.

Mandy's thoughts flew from Nipper to the foxes. She felt certain it was the same pair as the ones she and James had seen twice before. 'Where are they?' She bent down to peer through Mrs Ponsonby's car window.

'Somewhere up near the Beacon. Now dear, you must let me go. They need me to organise things. I should get up there in double-quick time!'

As Mrs Ponsonby drove off, James trotted back and picked up his bike. 'No sign,' he reported. Then he caught sight of Mandy's worried face. 'What's wrong?'

She gasped and gabbled out the news. 'They're going to shoot the foxes!' Surely by now Mrs Ponsonby must realise that was what Mr Western intended. She stared aghast at the disappearing car.

'Oh no they're not!' James said with fierce determination. He didn't even stop to think. 'Come on, Mandy. If we get up there before they do, we can scare the foxes away!'

She leaped into action after him. Soon they were pedalling furiously out of the village, up Moor Lane towards the Beacon. They ignored a wave from Walter Pickard outside the pub, and didn't even stop to talk to Mr Hope, who was driving back from a call at one of the farms on the moor.

'Where's the fire?' He stopped the car and leaned out, but Mandy and James sped by.

'Can't stop now!' Mandy called. They pedalled on. Breathless, their legs aching from the effort, they followed Mrs Ponsonby. Her car wound up the lane ahead of them and there, by the ancient stone cross, was a bunch of men, already gathered to take care of the foxes.

'See, they *have* got guns!' Mandy said, using her last ounce of energy. Five dark figures stood around, hands in pockets, long shotguns resting in the crooks of their arms. She could make out Major, Sam Western's big German shepherd, sniffing around at the base of the cross.

'Let's hope we're not too late!' Head down, James kept pedalling. 'We need to try and find out exactly where the foxes were last spotted. Then we can go and make as much noise as possible.'

'The men won't like it. They'll try and stop us,' Mandy warned. She wasn't scared of them and their guns, but she knew it wouldn't be easy. 'Look, they've spotted us!'

They saw Dennis Saville break away from the group and come towards them. He waved his arms and shouted at them to go away. Then there was another yell, and the men moved off quickly towards the brow of the hill, following Major as he picked up a scent. Mr Saville doubled back after them.

'Too late,' Mandy whispered. The dog had

definitely found a trail. He bounded out of sight on the far side of the hill. The gang of hunters broke into a run, then strung themselves out in a line on the horizon. They put their guns to their shoulders and aimed into the next valley.

But James refused to give in. 'Not yet, it isn't!' He ditched his bike and began to run across country.

Mandy knew there was nothing for it but to follow. She too flung down her bike and cut across the rough, heather-covered ground.

By this time Mrs Ponsonby did seem to have realised exactly what was going on. She got out of her car and began to protest. 'Mr Western, what on earth is happening? Why do you need those guns? My Fox Watch scheme is only meant to drive the foxes out of Welford. I didn't intend for you to come out and shoot them!'

The men ignored her. Her wailing voice was lost on the wind.

There was a sharp crack, then another and another. Puffs of smoke rose in the air as the guns went off. *Bang! Bang! Bang*! Mandy felt her heart jolt and shudder.

James came to a halt, his face suddenly white. He turned and stared at Mandy.

Mrs Ponsonby stood frozen to the spot. The dog barked, the men shouldered their guns, then dipped out of sight.

With stiff, leaden legs, James and Mandy forced themselves to follow, dreading what they would find when they crested the hill. The gunshots had cracked through the air and dashed their hopes.

'You were right.' James reached the top and stared down. 'We were too late.'

Mandy saw an animal lying quite still. It was almost too weak to move. Only the pure white tip of its bushy tail twitched feebly.

The men had scattered over the hillside, kicking at low bushes and peering under boulders where a fox might hide. They'd left their first quarry to bleed to death and were busy hunting down the second.

Mandy ran to the shot animal and crouched over it. It was the dog fox, wounded in the side, but still alive. His sides heaved, and a dark trickle of blood stained the ground.

Quickly she unwrapped her scarf from her neck and held it against the wound. 'We've got to stop the bleeding!' she insisted, as James came up beside her. 'If we can just do that, then maybe he stands a chance!'

The fox lay on his side, amber eyes staring up at her.

They were too shocked to notice another figure following them over the freezing ridge. The man ran quickly towards them, but it wasn't until he joined them by the injured fox that Mandy looked up and recognised her father. Behind him, she saw the stout figure of Mrs Ponsonby labouring up the hill.

'Let's have a look,' Adam Hope said quietly. He saw in a moment what had happened. He took the bloody scarf from Mandy and held it firmly in place, but he shook his head as he studied the fox. 'It's bad,' he warned. 'I don't think there's much we can do.'

Mandy bit back the tears. 'Try, Dad!'

He took off his jacket and covered the animal to keep it warm, but he knew from its condition that it was no good. 'I'm afraid he's bleeding internally as well.'

Helpless, they had to stand by and watch the fox die.

After what seemed like an age, the shuddering breaths stopped and the heaving sides were still.

Adam Hope leaned forward, closed the fox's eyes, then stood up. 'What about the vixen? Did she escape?'

'I think so.' James was the one who answered. He blinked hard and turned away from the body.

They stood staring down at the half-dozen men who had killed the fox. The hunters searched on for the vixen, but Major had lost the scent and was zigzagging aimlessly across the hill.

'They don't care! They left him to suffer and die!' Mandy cried. Tears streamed down her cheeks. She choked and couldn't say any more.

Adam Hope took up the dead fox and went to meet Mrs Ponsonby before the men returned. Mandy felt herself being helped gently into the

Animal Ark Land-rover, but she was in a daze. She hardly knew where she was or who was there, only that a dreadful thing had happened.

Nothing could make her feel better, not her dad's kind words, nor Mrs Ponsonby's heartfelt apologies, nor her mum's comforting arms when they arrived at Animal Ark late in the afternoon.

Mandy told her what had happened.

They were hard facts, dragged out from the depths of her own suffering: 'Oh, Mum, one fox had been shot dead, and the other is being hunted up on the moor. And to make things worse, poor Nipper is lost in the freezing cold!'

Five

'Mum says the vixen probably went safely to earth,' Mandy told her grandfather next morning. He'd called to persuade her out of the house to help him put the finishing touches to the lights in the village square. It was Thursday, and Joe Wortley was due to switch them on at seven-thirty the next evening.

'We can't have you moping about the house when there's so much to do,' he'd insisted.

'I don't feel much like it, Grandad.' Mandy had hardly slept. She felt washed out and unhappy, unable to get the picture of the dead fox out of her mind.

'Come on, the fresh air will do you good. I've had strict orders from your gran not to let you get away with saying no!'

So, to please her grandparents, she'd wrapped up in her jacket, scarf and hat and come to help. The tall Christmas tree stood outside the door of the Fox and Goose, opposite the church. It rose almost as high as the roof of the pub, with coloured lights strung through its branches.

'Well then, at least one of the foxes lives to fight another day,' her grandad said now, standing back to judge the effect of the lights in the tree. 'Adam tells me he knew something was badly wrong the moment he saw you and James hurtling up the hill on your bikes. He decided he'd better follow and see what was up.'

'I'm glad he did.' she sighed. 'If Dad hadn't come, I'd always have wondered if there was anything we could have done to save the fox.' Her lip quivered as she remembered the wounded fox's amber eyes staring up at her.

Just then, a Range Rover cruised down the main street into the pub carpark. Mandy saw Joe Wortley and Sophie Dixon get out. The television star went into the Fox and Goose, leaving Sophie to cross the road and head for home by herself. When she saw Mandy, she ducked her head and rushed on.

'Watch out!' Mandy yelled, as another car sped by. Sophie had been so busy ignoring her that she hadn't seen it. The driver braked hard and skidded as Sophie stepped back. An accident had been narrowly avoided.

'Are you OK?' Mandy ran across.

'Fine, thanks.' The girl's pale face had turned bright red. 'I just wasn't looking where I was going.'

An alarmed driver glared out of his window at her before he straightened his car and drove off. Mandy's grandad watched from a distance to see that everything was all right.

'Have you found Nipper yet?' The question popped out before Mandy had time to think. Since Sophie had been doing her best to avoid her, it was obvious that she didn't want to talk about the lost puppy.

She shook her head and the curtain of black, shiny hair swung across her face. 'I've looked everywhere.'

'I'm sorry about his eyesight,' Mandy said quietly.

This time Sophie nodded once. 'Thanks.' She bit her lip. 'Would this disease hurt? I mean, would he be in pain with it?'

Mandy answered as best she could. 'I don't think so. It just makes his vision go blurred. Why?'

'Nothing. I was wondering, that's all.' Sophie changed the subject. 'We found a home for Olivia this morning. That's the last of the puppies. She went with her new owners after breakfast.' She put on a cheerful smile. 'Well, I'd better go now.'

'No, listen!' Mandy walked with her across the road. 'About Nipper; have your parents really made up their minds about him?' She still clung on to a shred of hope that the puppy might be found.

'Mummy has. She says it would be much too much trouble to look after a handicapped dog. She rang someone who breeds rough collies at the place where we bought Henrietta. The man there said that pups with collie eye should definitely not be allowed to breed.'

'But that's not the same as having him put to sleep!' Mandy insisted. 'Anyway, Henrietta is the one who passed it on to Nipper. According to this man, he should never have sold Henrietta to you in the first place!'

'Try telling Mummy that.' Sophie shrugged and walked on down the path. 'Anyway, it's beside the point now. Nipper ran away and that's all there is to it.'

'It was minus three degrees last night.' Mandy had checked the thermometer, as usual. 'If he was out in the open, you realise what could have happened to him?'

Sophie rounded on her. 'I know! You don't need to tell me!'

'Sorry.' Mandy stepped back.

'Look, he ran away, OK? I let him off the lead to play, and the next thing I knew he'd vanished! I looked everywhere for him but I couldn't find him!' Sophie glared angrily at Mandy.

'Where were you when it happened?' In her own mind, she began to plan another search. She would call at James's house. Together they would try again.

'Out of the village somewhere, by a big house. Oh, I don't know!'

'Which house? Was it up on the moor or down by the river?' Mandy put her hand on Sophie's arm.

'Like I said, just out of the village. I don't know the name of it, do I? I've only just moved in here!' She turned away to shake Mandy off.

'Sorry, I didn't mean to upset you,' she murmured. Sophie obviously cared about Nipper, but she seemed edgy and secretive.

'Look, leave me alone, will you! It's bad enough without having to answer all these questions.' Her grey eyes flashed out a warning. 'The way you're all going on about it, anyone would think I'd lost Nipper on purpose!'

Sophie's bad temper only made Mandy more determined to carry on with the search. She went back to help her grandfather put the finishing touches to the tree, but all the time she was making plans.

'What's going on inside that head of yours?' Grandad Hope asked as they slid his stepladders into the back of his camper-van, ready to drive back to Lilac Cottage.

'What do you mean?' She blushed and smiled.

'You're too quiet for my liking. It usually means you're up to something.'

'Me?' Mandy didn't mind being teased. As she climbed into the passenger seat, she decided to tell him all about Nipper, knowing that he would understand.

'That's a hard one,' he admitted. He cleared the steamed-up windscreen and turned the ignition key. 'I've never even heard of collie eye. They always look such a fit and active type of dog.'

Before they set off for home, he turned to look at her. 'Do I take it you're going to carry on with the search?'

She nodded. 'I'll give James a ring after lunch and see if he wants to come too.'

'No need. Here he comes now.' Grandad pointed to a figure speeding down the main street on a bike. 'It looks like he's just come from your place and he's in a mighty big hurry.'

James squealed to a halt beside the van. 'Your mum said I'd find you here!' he gasped. 'I was looking for you in case you wanted to come out and look for Nipper with me!'

Mandy grinned. 'Great minds think alike.'

'But listen, something else has come up.' He hardly paused for breath. 'It's Mrs Ponsonby. I think she's gone fox-mad!'

'Oh no, not again!' Mandy's heart sank. As if it wasn't enough that the bossy, interfering lady had already been partly to blame for one fox's death. 'What's happened now?'

'She's just brought Pandora into the surgery with an injured paw. She's going on and on about a fox attacking the dog, demanding to see a vet, telling everyone it's an emergency.'

Mandy drew a deep breath. 'Not again! Did she

actually *see* a fox attack Pandora this time?'

James shrugged. 'I don't even know how bad the paw is. When I saw Pandora, her foot was wrapped up in a big towel. Jean took the dog straight into a treatment room, partly to stop Mrs Ponsonby making such a fuss. Mr Saville was in the waiting-room with Major. I noticed him listening to Mrs Ponsonby to find out what was going on, then he got up and left. I came straight down here to let you know.' He pushed his hair from his forehead and breathed at last.

'What do you want to do; go ahead and look for Nipper, or go back and sort Mrs Ponsonby out first?' Grandad could see that Mandy was torn between two missions.

'Animal Ark,' she decided, thanking James and telling him to sling his bike into the back of the camper-van and climb in. 'It'll only take a few minutes to find out what's happening. I'm worried about Dennis Saville as well,' she confessed. 'We don't want Mr Western and his men poking their noses in again.'

So they chugged off in the camper-van, arriving at the surgery just as Emily Hope emerged from the treatment room to give Mrs Ponsonby news of Pandora's injury.

'How is she?' Mrs Ponsonby cried. 'How is my poor precious darling?'

'She's going to be OK. It isn't a deep cut, so she doesn't even need stitches. I've cleaned it up and left Simon to strap it up with a bandage.' Mrs Hope stood with her hands in the pockets of her white coat. She glanced up at Mandy and gave her a smile as she came in.

'Not a deep cut?' Mrs Ponsonby quizzed. 'Are you sure? There was an awful lot of blood!'

'Not really. It looked worse than it was.'

'But Pandora was attacked by a fox! And they have such sharp, vicious teeth.'

Emily Hope put her head to one side. 'A fox?'

'Certainly. There's no doubt about it. I heard a dreadful noise of clattering out in the stable yard, so I knew the greedy creatures had come back to raid my bins. I got there just in time to rescue poor Pandora from serious injury!'

'Hmm. It doesn't look like the sort of injury a fox would inflict, Mrs Ponsonby. The cut is too clean for a start. A fox would tear the flesh in a more jagged way. No, I'd say this was done by a sharp edge; something like the rim of a tin, for instance.'

Mrs Ponsonby sniffed and shook her head. 'No.

It was the fox who got away from Mr Western's men yesterday, I'm convinced of it. To tell you the truth, the fox scares me. Living alone in my big house isn't easy. Any sudden noise or unwelcome visitor is very alarming, especially at night. And of course, poor Pandora and Toby are frightened of him too.'

'Her,' Mandy said quietly.

Everyone turned to look.

'Pardon?' the fussy old lady said.

'Her. It's a vixen. The dog fox is dead.'

'Well, whatever.' Mrs Ponsonby squared her shoulders and prepared for battle. 'As soon as I can get Pandora safely tucked up in her basket at Bleakfell Hall, I'll be on the phone, organising my Fox Watch group to drive the pest out once and for all!'

Six

'She means it, Mandy!' James tried to yell over his shoulder as they pedalled hard for Bleakfell Hall. 'Mrs Ponsonby is dead set on chasing the vixen out of the village!'

'Not if we have anything to do with it.' Mandy gritted her teeth. 'Anyway, it's not Mrs Ponsonby I'm worried about. It's Mr Saville and Mr Western.' The farm manager must have rushed back to Upper Welford Hall to tell his boss where the fox was now. It was vital for her and James to get to Bleakfell Hall before they did.

Given Dennis Saville's long drive up Moor Lane, that shouldn't be too difficult, she decided. Once they reached the gateway to Mrs Ponsonby's old house with its towers and tall chimneys, she slowed down. She gazed up at the crumbling stone walls and arched windows and noticed Toby barking madly from a downstairs room. 'It's OK; we made it,' she gasped, glancing back down the road for Mr Western's car. 'No one's here yet.'

'Let's go round the back and take a look.' James dismounted and pushed his bike past the stone steps leading to the old doorway. 'Didn't Mrs Ponsonby say that the fox comes to raid her dustbins in the stable yard?'

Mandy nodded. The back of the Hall was even more run down than the front. A door to an outhouse had come off its hinges and stood propped against the wall, and long icicles had formed on the leaking gutters. 'This place gives me the creeps,' she muttered.

'Look, those must be the stables.' James pointed to a row of divided doors shut and bolted at top and bottom. They hid their bikes behind a wall and went cautiously across the yard. 'I wonder when they last had any horses in them?'

'Centuries ago, by the look of it.' Mandy shivered. The yard was covered in a thick frost, and in one corner she spotted the dustbins. 'See!'

She pointed to a row of rusty, old-fashioned metal bins. Some of the lids were missing, and one was tipped on to its side.

'What a mess.' James frowned. Scraps of paper blew here and there, a tin can rolled and knocked against a wall.

'Wait a minute!' Mandy had gone to take a closer look. As she bent to stand the bin upright, she noticed tracks in the frost. 'James, look! Footprints!'

He ran across to study the light marks, the padded foot and sharp nails of the animal that had raided the bin. 'What kind are they?'

Mandy looked twice, then three times. She had to be sure. The footprints were delicate. The creature was small and dog-like. There were also marks where a long tail might have brushed the ground. 'They're fox-prints,' she whispered with a sinking heart.

'It looks like Mrs Ponsonby was right, then.' Here was the evidence in front of them. James sighed. 'Now we can't keep on saying the fox is innocent.'

'So what? She's only doing what comes naturally. Wouldn't you take advantage of what people threw away if you were a fox? Mandy stuck up for animals against people as usual. 'What harm does it do?'

'Hang on, I'm not arguing with you.' James only half listened. 'There's a spot of dried blood in this corner and another one by the bin! I wonder how they got there.'

But then he picked up another set of tracks. 'Mandy, come and look at these. They're different!'

She followed him towards the stable doors. The new tracks were more scuffed. This time the shape of each footprint was human. The prints led straight to the peeling door of the stable furthest from the house. 'Whoever it is, they're still in there!' Mandy breathed. The tracks stopped at the door and didn't come out.

'How did they get in in the first place?' James tried the door. The bottom half was bolted from the outside.

'Through here?' She took hold of the top half of the door and felt it swing open with a loud creak. 'Watch your head, James!'

He ducked just in time. 'What now?'

'Listen, did you hear something?' Mandy peered into the dark, musty stable. Her voice echoed in the empty space. 'A kind of whine. There it is again! She braced her arms against the bottom section of the stable door and got ready to vault over.

'It sounds scared,' James whispered.

'It's not the only one!' As her eyes grew used to the dark, Mandy made out a heap of old straw in one corner of the stable. There was a rusty manger and old bridles hanging from hooks on the wall. Above her head, a loft ran the length of the rough, disused building. As she looked up, a dusty cobweb brushed her face and made her jump.

'Hang on, I'm coming in after you.' James jumped over the door and followed. 'Mandy, are you thinking what I'm thinking?'

The whining grew louder. It was definitely coming from the pile of straw. '. . . That it might not be the fox?' Small furry footprints, a whining noise turning to a yelp as they crept towards the corner. 'Nipper?' she said softly.

The straw rustled and shifted, then a tall figure stood up out of the untidy heap. Sophie Dixon glared at them. She held a squirming puppy in her arms. 'What do you want now, Mandy Hope?' she demanded in an angry, scornful voice. 'Why can't you mind your own business just for once?'

'We want to help,' James said, once he got over his surprise and Mandy had introduced him to Sophie and Nipper. 'You don't need to worry, we're on your side.'

'You won't tell anybody I lied?' Sophie set the puppy down in his straw bed.

'No. But how did you find this place?' James wanted to know the full story.

'I didn't. Nipper did. He did run away when we were out on our walk; that part was true. But I didn't lose him, I followed him here. I think he could smell the left-overs in the dustbins, so he sneaked in through the back gate. I was going to tell him off and taken him home, then it just came to me in a flash: why not hide him here? No one would know. I could come secretly every day and look after him. It would have worked too, if you two hadn't barged in.'

'I can see why you did it,' Mandy said slowly. For the first time she saw that Sophie Dixon was nicer than she seemed. Anyone who went out of their way to help an animal was OK in her book. 'But what did you think you could do in the long run? I mean, you can't keep Nipper locked away in Mrs Ponsonby's stable for ever.'

'Why not?' said Sophie still resenting their interference.

'Well, for a start, he needs fresh air and exercise.'

'I can come and take him for walks without being seen, can't I?'

'But he needs special care because of his eyesight. And he needs company. He's going to be lonely in here all by himself.'

Sophie sighed. She had no answer to this. 'OK, if you're so clever, what would you have done?' She turned on Mandy.

It was Mandy's turn to shake her head and sigh. Suddenly a lot of things slotted into place: the reason why Henrietta and Olivia had arrived back at the vicarage before Sophie, the fact that Sophie's shoes had been covered in mud and straw. And hadn't Mrs Dixon said that her daughter had been upset by the news about Nipper? But still, finding her here with him now came as a complete surprise. Mandy bent to stroke the puppy, giving herself time to decide what they should do next.

'I did it to save Nipper's life!' Sophie pleaded. 'If you give us away now, they'll do what they were going to do in the first place!'

'It's OK, I've already said we won't tell.' James stepped in again. 'Will we, Mandy?'

She felt the puppy's rough tongue lick her hand. 'What if he needs treatment?' she said quietly. She didn't know enough about collie eye to be sure

that it was safe to leave it untreated.

'You told me yourself he wouldn't be in any pain!' Sophie flashed back at her, taking Nipper into her own arms.

'Yes, but I can't tell if it'll get any worse. We know that he can still see a bit, it's true, but Mum would be able to tell us more if we asked her.'

'No!' came the quick, fierce answer.

'OK, not yet at any rate.' James stepped in between them. 'Listen, you two, I think I just heard a car coming up the drive!' He put his hands up and warned them not to go on arguing.

'You're right!' Mandy listened to the crunch of car tyres over gravel. 'But it doesn't sound like Mrs Ponsonby.' The noise of the engine was deep; more like a Land-rover than the little runabout used by the owner of Bleakfell Hall.

'Mr Western?' James craned his head over the stable door to investigate. 'It's no good. I can't see!'

'You'd better hide Nipper,' Mandy urged Sophie. As she helped to cover them both with straw, she explained why they suspected the landowner and his manager might have come in search of the fox.

'Shh! I can hear voices!' James pulled the door closed. Now they were in total darkness. The straw rustled, Nipper whimpered, while Sophie calmed him. 'Try to keep him quiet,' James warned.

Mandy went to join him. 'What can you hear now?'

'Men. At least two of them. Listen, you can hear them talking.'

Car doors slammed, footsteps came round the side of the house. There was the faint sound of Toby barking from inside the house. Then Mandy too heard them speak.

'. . . Not back from the vets' yet.'

'It makes no difference. If she says the fox was here, she'd want us to take a look.'

Now Mandy knew that James had been right. It was Dennis Saville and Sam Western. Their heavy feet tramped into the stone-flagged yard.

The muffled voices of the two men grew louder. She heard Dennis Saville give a short laugh. 'After yesterday, I'm not so sure. She didn't sound too happy when she saw us with the guns.'

'Well, what did she expect? I suppose she thinks you can track down a fox and ask him politely if he'd mind leaving the premises!' Mr Western was scornful as he poked about amongst the bins. 'There's been a fox here all right.'

Mandy held her breath. *Please let Nipper keep quiet*! Now the footsteps approached the stables.

'And something else by the look of it.' Dennis Saville's gruff voice was right outside the door. 'These prints here are more like a dog's. Hey, wait a minute!'

James and Mandy prayed hard.

'These are human footprints too!' Saville had spotted the new set of prints made when Mandy and James had investigated the stable.

It would only be seconds before the two men tried the door, moments until they were discovered. Now all they could hope was that they could bluff their way through without giving Sophie away. They gritted their teeth and prepared themselves.

Just then, another car drove up and stopped. It made the two men hesitate.

'It sounds like the Fox Watch lady herself,' Sam Western muttered. 'She'll have seen our car. I suppose we'd better go and tell her where we are and what we're doing here.'

But before they could get halfway across the yard, Mandy heard Pandora's excited yap. She pictured the little Pekinese hurtling round the side of the house, bandaged leg or not. 'Down!' Mr Western said roughly, as Pandora barked and growled.

Then Mrs Ponsonby came into the yard, hot on the heels of her angry pet. 'Mr Western, Mr Saville, put those guns down!'

James allowed himself a big sigh of relief as Mrs Ponsonby's loud voice echoed off the walls. Mandy could just see his face in the gloom. 'Phew!' she whispered. Behind them, Sophie and Nipper shifted position under the straw.

'We heard the fox was back,' Sam Western began.

'But did you hear me ask for your help?' Mrs Ponsonby demanded.

Pandora yapped and snarled, and now they could hear Toby's rougher bark as a back door was unlocked and the mongrel came bounding out of the house.

'No, but Dennis here heard about your problem at the vets' this morning. Naturally we thought . . .'

'Well, you thought wrong, Mr Western. I'm not a violent woman, and I certainly don't believe in guns. If I'd thought that you intended to employ them, I would never have included you in my Fox Watch scheme!'

'Good for her!' James whispered. His eyes glinted and he smiled at Mandy.

'We're farmers, Mrs Ponsonby. What did you expect?'

'Knowledge and expertise, Mr Western. Not brute force!' Obviously Mrs Ponsonby could stand her ground. 'Down, Toby! Down, Pandora! Now, you will please do as I request and put away your guns.'

'What about the fox?' Dennis Saville made one last appeal.

Mandy pictured Mrs Ponsonby drawing herself

up to full height in her bright red winter coat and hat. There was a long pause before she gave her reply. 'As leader of Welford Fox Watch scheme, rest assured, Mr Saville, you can leave this fox to me!'

Seven

'That was close!' James waited until they heard the sound of the landowner's car making its way back up Mrs Ponsonby's drive. Then he went to tell Sophie it was safe to come out.

She emerged with her hair in a mess and bits of straw sticking out of her polo-neck sweater. 'Why is everyone going on about this fox? What's so special about it?'

Mandy explained that the vixen's partner had been killed by the farmers the day before. 'We don't want the same thing to happen to this one. In fact, we'd do anything to save her!' As she spoke, she watched Sophie's face closely. Once more she got the feeling that the girl knew more than she was saying. Her grey eyes had the same guarded look as they'd had when she'd lied about the lost puppy. She turned her head sideways and pretended to be interested in something in the far corner of the stable.

'What would you do to save her?' she challenged when Mandy had finished.

'Anything!' Mandy repeated. 'Why?' She saw from James's frown that he was as puzzled as she was.

'Hang on a minute!' Sophie went to the door and opened it a fraction of an inch. 'All clear,' she whispered. 'Mrs Ponsonby has taken those noisy dogs of hers into the house. It doesn't look as if she's going to come snooping around in here, thank heavens.' She drew a slim silver torch from her pocket and turned it on.

For some reason, Sophie Dixon had begun to annoy Mandy once more. Perhaps it was her secretive expression. To Mandy's surprise, she found herself sticking up for Mrs Ponsonby. 'I'd have thought she had the right to snoop around inside her own stables!' she retorted, ignoring James's astonished look. 'And Toby and Pandora aren't any noisier than other dogs would be if they saw strange men in their garden!'

'OK, OK, keep your hair on.' Sophie shone the torch towards the rickety wooden loft above their heads. 'I don't know why you're defending her. Isn't she the one who wants to get rid of your precious fox?'

'At least she doesn't want her killed!' Mandy felt herself go hot. If it hadn't been for the fact that she didn't want to dash off without solving the Nipper problem, she wouldn't have stayed in the stable a moment longer.

'Look, do you want to save this fox, or not?'

'Of course we do.'

'You're not acting as if you do.'

'Why, what do you know about her?'

'More than you think.'

'Ha!' Mandy turned away exasperated. What was the point of trying to carry on a conversation with someone as difficult as Sophie Dixon?

James's frown deepened. 'Why are you shining the torch up there?' The yellow beam swung across the roof and down on to an ancient ladder that led from ground level to the loft.

Sophie turned it on his face. James's glasses glinted in the light, as he put his hand up to shield his eyes. 'If Mandy would just stop arguing, I could show you something.'

'What?' Mandy demanded.

'Shh! You'll have to be quiet.' She clicked off the torch and slid it back in her pocket. 'Otherwise she might not come out.'

Plunged into sudden darkness again, they stood and waited. Mandy felt the puppy come sniffing round her ankles, but she hardly noticed. 'Who might not come out?' she whispered urgently.

'Guess.' Sophie spun it out as long as she could.

'The fox,' James supplied the answer in a low whisper. 'You've seen her up there in the loft, haven't you?'

'Twice. Last night and earlier this morning. She's still up there now, only you two have probably frightened her into hiding.'

For a few moments there was silence. Was it true? Or was Sophie having a cruel joke at their expense? The more she thought about it, the more Mandy could see how the vixen might have fled down from the moor after the shock of seeing her partner killed. Maybe she would hole up in a dark, deserted place like this. After all, she knew she would be safe from the farmers, and she could keep warm and dry. And then there were the prints in the frost by the dustbins, and Mrs Ponsonby's claim that a fox had attacked Pandora.

'Don't you believe me?' Sophie whispered. 'Well, come and see.'

She led the way up the ladder, knowing that they would follow. James went next, putting one foot on the rickety bottom rung. 'Are you coming, Mandy?' he whispered.

Mandy nodded and followed. The ladder creaked. She heard Sophie reach the top and step into the loft. If the fox was up there, she would certainly know she was being cornered. She might be frightened and perhaps try a sudden, wild dash for freedom. Yet the only way down was by the ladder. Mandy climbed as quickly as she could, anxious to get it over with.

'Wait here.' Sophie ordered them to stay by the ladder. 'We don't want her to escape.'

They crouched under the rafters, able to make out an old stack of hay bales in one corner. 'Is that what she uses as her den?' James asked.

Sophie nodded. 'You should see her climb up here. She moves like lightning.'

He turned to Mandy. 'I can smell her, can you?'

Taking a deep breath, Mandy's nostrils filled with a sharp, unmistakeable stink. She knew then that Sophie had been telling the truth.

Then she heard a rustle of straw, and saw the

tip of a pair of pointed black ears. There were bright orange eyes staring at them through the darkness, a long snout, a flash of white chest as the fox eased its head from behind one of the bales.

'Come on, let's go down!' James had seen enough. 'We're scaring her.'

Fumbling, half-slipping, they made their way down the ladder. Nipper greeted them by dashing and barging straight into their legs, tangling himself up in feet and straw. Sophie picked him up and dusted him down.

'What do you say now?' There was a small grin on her face as she confronted James and Mandy.

'I'd say she chose a pretty good place to lie up and rest,' James said. 'Except that now we know she's here.'

'Yes, but none of us is going to give her away!' Mandy said. Then she stopped short. 'Are we?' She looked from James to Sophie, her eyes widening into a stare. 'Oh no!' There had to be a reason for Sophie showing them the fox's hiding-place, and at that moment Mandy knew exactly what it was.

Sophie stared her out. 'That's right. You said you'd do anything to save the fox. Well, I won't give her away if you promise not to tell a single soul about Nipper!'

It was blackmail, but James and Mandy had to agree.

'I feel dreadful. Nipper oughtn't to be locked up in that dark stable,' Mandy said as they cycled back into the village.

'No, but I suppose I can see why she's doing it,' James answered quietly. 'She's trying to save his life.'

Mandy thought about it. 'He's safe for today, and so is the fox, as long as we don't say anything. But what about tomorrow? What's going to happen in the long run?'

'I don't think Sophie knows yet. But from the way she's behaving, I'd say she was pretty desperate. She can only take it one day at a time.'

As they reached the village square, Mandy stopped and sighed. 'This is what you'd call stalemate, isn't it?'

James nodded. 'At least the fox is safe,' he repeated.

'If Sophie keeps her word.'

'She will.' He sounded sure of this much.

* * *

So they cycled off on their different ways home.
By the time Mandy reached Animal Ark and
passed her mum on her way out of the surgery,
she was still feeling confused.

'How do the Christmas lights look?' Emily
Hope asked.

'What? Oh, fine, thanks.' Mandy went straight
into the house to find her dad cooking soup
for lunch.

He handed her a steaming bowl and a hunk of
crusty bread. 'Eat this, it'll warm you up.'

'Oh, OK, thanks, Dad.' Mandy sat and picked
up her spoon, then paused with it midway to her
mouth. 'Dad, is it cruel to keep a blind dog alive?'

'It depends on the circumstances. Why do
you ask?'

'No special reason.' She reddened and put
down her spoon without eating. 'But when would
it be cruel?'

'Only when the condition causing the blindness
is painful for the dog. Dogs have excellent hearing
and sense of smell, as you know. That makes up
for their loss of eyesight. You can still take a blind
dog for walks. He'll probably want to stay pretty
close to you, and you have to be patient and
understanding. You have to speak to the dog more

often than usual, so he can get his bearings, and so that he's not too lonely.'

'Hmm.' Mandy narrowed her eyes and stared out of the window at the frosty scene.

Mr Hope studied her face. 'Come on, love, what's up?'

'Nothing, Dad, honestly.'

'Yes, there is. I can tell. Has it got anything to do with the rough collie pup – what's his name? Zippy, Nippy . . . Nipper, that's it!'

Mandy ducked her head and pretended to blow on her hot soup.

'I thought he'd gone missing. The Dixons didn't seem to have tried too hard to find him, poor little chap.' Again he looked closely at her. 'Mandy?'

'I can't say anything, Dad. I promised.' Now she kicked herself for bringing the subject up in the first place.

Adam Hope sat down opposite her. He waited a while before he spoke again. 'Listen, Mandy, I don't know exactly what the problem is here. But it looks like you've got yourself into a situation you'd rather not be in. Is that right?'

Tears gathered as she looked up and nodded. Her dad was being kind again. 'Stop it, or I'll cry,' she warned.

Mr Hope dipped into his pocket and handed her a big hankie. 'Blow your nose on that. That should cure it.' He wrinkled his nose and grinned. 'Better? Oh dear, I feel a piece of good advice coming on. Do you mind?'

She dabbed and sniffed. 'No. Go ahead.'

'Well, then. Don't take on too much responsibility. If this has got something to do with rescuing another animal in trouble and you find that for once you can't solve the problem by yourself, or even with James's level-headed help, then maybe it's best just to take a step back and let someone else help to sort it out instead.' He spoke gently, without prying or trying to boss her. 'After all, it is nearly Christmas!'

'That makes it worse.' *Poor little Nipper, alone in the cold stable.*

'And you're sure there's nothing we can do?'

'Thanks, Dad, but no.' Mandy stood up without touching her soup. 'Do you mind if I don't eat it? My tummy feels all knotted up.'

'It sounds like a hard promise you made back there!'

'It is,' she sighed. 'Very hard. As a matter of fact, two lives depend on it!'

Eight

'Hello, Mrs Dixon. Is Sophie in, please?' Mandy stood at the door of the Old Vicarage. In the background she could see Henrietta plodding from room to room, looking as if she'd lost something.

'Hello. It's Mandy, isn't it?' Helena Dixon looked harassed. 'As a matter of fact, she isn't. She was here for lunch, but then she slipped out again. She's behaving very oddly at the moment.'

'How come?' Mandy was disappointed. It had taken a lot of nerve to face coming here to talk to Sophie again. A dozen times she'd changed her mind; yes, it would do some good, then no it wouldn't, then yes it would.

'Well, this morning, for instance, I asked if she wanted to come to Walton to go Christmas shopping with me, and she said no. That's not at all like Sophie; she loves shopping. Then after lunch I wanted her to take Henrietta out for a walk, but when I went to look for her in the TV room, she wasn't there. Now I've no idea where she is.'

I bet I do, Mandy thought. But she said nothing.

'Poor Henrietta's been moping since the last pup left for her new home. I thought a walk would do her good.' She looked hard at Mandy. 'I don't suppose you would take her for me? Of course, I'd pay whatever you normally charge.'

'I'll do it for nothing, 'Mandy said promptly.

'Are you sure? Wouldn't you like some extra pocket money for last-minute Christmas presents?' Mrs Dixon had already lifted the dog-lead off its hook by the door. Henrietta came bounding across the hallway in a flurry of white, black and brown fur.

'No thanks. How long do you want me to keep her?'

'Well, I've promised to pop back to Walton to meet Joe and Andrew, my husband. Would it be all right if you brought Henrietta back in a couple of hours?'

They made the arrangements, then Mandy and Henrietta set off, up by the church and down the main street. The dog wasn't especially big, but she was strong, Mandy found. She pulled at the lead, dodging into gateways and sniffing at corners. 'Hey, who's taking who for a walk?' she cried, when Henrietta spotted Ernie Bell's cat, Tiddles, and shot across the road after him. She barked and tugged, almost pulling Mandy off her feet.

Tiddles waited until the last moment, then zoomed off, up the path to his home at the end of a short row of terraced houses.

Ernie's grizzled head appeared round his front door. 'Can't you keep that dog under control?' he yelled. 'Oh, Mandy, it's you. I hope you're taking that wayward dog in hand and giving it a few lessons in how to behave. It's been a real menace to Tiddles ever since it came to live in the vicarage.'

Mandy gathered her breath as Henrietta jumped up at the gate and rattled it with her front paws. 'Sorry, Ernie. I'm supposed to be taking her for a walk, but it's turning out to be the other way round!' It was true; Henrietta certainly needed some proper training. 'It's not her fault, though. She's a lovely dog, deep down!'

'And I'm Santa Claus,' the old man grumbled, disappearing indoors again.

'Take no notice, young miss,' Walter Pickard chipped in. Walter lived four doors down from Ernie. 'You know what he's like; always grabbing the chance to have a good moan. Especially at Christmas time.' He winked at Mandy and grinned at the unruly dog. 'Mind you, you have got your hands full there.'

Henrietta wanted to be off. She was straining at the lead, almost pulling Mandy's arm out of its socket.

'She doesn't get enough exercise,' Mandy gasped. She staggered down the street, slipping and sliding on the frosty pavement. 'See you soon, Walter!'

'Tomorrow night!' he promised. 'That's when they have this big do to switch on the lights, isn't it?'

'Will Ernie be there too?' It seemed as if the whole village was coming.

'You bet he will. As soon as he heard they were handing out free mince-pies, he made up his mind to be first in the queue. When did you ever hear of Ernie turning down something for nothing?'

'Now just hang on a minute . . .'

Mandy heard Ernie's door reopen and the old

grumbler's gruff voice start up again. She would let them sort it out between them, she decided. Anyway, Henrietta was well on her way to McFarlanes' post office, and she couldn't have stopped her if she'd wanted to.

'Hi, James, hi, Blackie!' Mandy waved at them as they came out of the shop.

'Whoa!' James yelled. 'Where are you off to?'

'I don't know. It doesn't look as if it's up to me!' Henrietta charged on.

'Can we come anyway?' James and Blackie quickly caught up. James glanced at Mandy's hot face and windswept hair. 'Did you volunteer to do this?' he asked.

'Kind of.' Mandy began to think that Henrietta had picked up a trail. 'I called at her house to talk to Sophie again.'

'About Nipper?'

'Yes. I wanted to try and persuade her to take him back home.' In spite of her dad's advice, Mandy still felt she had to do something. The idea of leaving the puppy in Mrs Ponsonby's dark stable gnawed away at her. 'I thought that if I talked to her again, she might listen to reason!'

For a few moments James said nothing. 'But she wasn't there?' he asked.

'No. I think I can guess where she is, though.'

'It looks like Henrietta knows, too.' James saw how the dog pulled at her lead, nose to the ground. They were heading out of the village now, towards Bleakfell Hall. 'Mandy, do you think we ought to risk it? What if Sophie's there when we arrive? She'll think we've broken our promise.'

Mandy was determined. 'Why should she? We could be going to check that the fox is still OK, for all she knows.'

'But we're not, are we?'

'Yes, in a way.' Mandy couldn't separate the fox from the puppy. She felt somehow that their fates were linked.

'James, I've talked to Dad, and he says even a blind puppy can be trained to live a good life. You don't have to put them down just because they can't see. And Nipper isn't even completely blind! But if we try to tell the Dixons that, Sophie will say we've broken our promise, and she'll tell Mrs Ponsonby about our fox. I've gone over and over it, and in the end I decided that the only thing we could do was get Sophie to persuade her mum and dad to let her take Nipper home after all.'

'Just like that?' James said doubtfully. He kept

Blackie on the lead as they came within sight of the big gates leading to Bleakfell Hall.

Mandy pulled hard on Henrietta's lead and managed to make her stop. They stayed hidden behind the high garden wall. 'Have you got a better idea?' she asked.

'Well, I suppose we can't leave Nipper in the stable much longer,' James admitted. 'I've been thinking about the poor little thing ever since we left her there with Sophie this morning.'

'Me too. Dad says blind dogs need even more company than normal dogs, otherwise they get lonely and miserable.' It was getting harder to hang on to Henrietta as they talked it through. The dog snuffled at the gatepost, nosing here and there in the grass and flower borders.

James stood on tiptoe and peered over the wall. 'Mrs Ponsonby's car's in the drive,' he reported. 'And the lights are on in the house. That means she's at home.'

'Yes, and Sophie's probably in the stable with Nipper right now as well,' Mandy reminded him. She didn't think she had the strength to hold Henrietta back much longer. 'I'm going down the side of the garden to take a proper look. Are you coming?'

James followed, careful not to let Blackie make any noise. They had to crouch and creep forward, out of sight of the downstairs windows of the Hall, in case Toby and Pandora were on guard. Their feet crunched over frozen leaves in the ditch. Low branches that hung over the garden wall snared them and caught in their hair.

'Henrietta can hardly wait to see Nipper again.' Mandy whispered, as she felt the dog pull and strain. 'I'm sure she's picked up the scent, James!'

He nodded. 'See that double gate?' They turned a corner round the back of the house and its grounds and looked along the length of another stretch of wall. 'That must lead into the stable yard. We might be able to get in there without being seen.'

Mandy guessed that it was the entrance Sophie had been using, too.

'It's OK, we can stand up straight now,' James said. The wall was tall enough for them to run freely towards the gate without being seen.

'Only one more minute!' Mandy promised the impatient Henrietta. Then they would be in the yard and safely across into the disused stable.

Her heart raced, her arms ached as she glanced

at James, and the two dogs came to a sudden halt outside the gate.

'What is it, Blackie?' James whispered. The dog cocked one ear and whined. 'What did you hear?'

'Henrietta heard it too,' Mandy said. They froze to the spot and waited. 'Listen, there's someone in the yard!'

'Or *something*.' James strained to pick up where the noise was coming from. 'That sounds like a dustbin lid being tipped open.'

Mandy heard the scrape of metal, and then a sudden clang as the lid clattered to the ground. She stared at the peeling paint of the tall double gate, as if she might suddenly develop X-ray vision and stare right through it. There, in the bare, frosty yard, the phantom raider of Mrs Ponsonby's dustbins was hard at work.

A bin tipped and rolled with a hollow thud. They could hear waste paper being kicked aside, and the lighter rattle of empty cans.

'It's the fox. She must be hungry,' James hissed. His breath blew clouds of steam into the cold air. He put a hand on Blackie's neck to quieten him.

Henrietta looked up at Mandy from under her long fringe of grey and white fur. She gave a high whine. 'Shh!' Mandy dropped to her knees on the frost-covered grass to talk to the dog. 'We know you want to see Nipper, but just wait until the fox has finished her dinner.'

Henrietta's whine deepened to a growl. She couldn't understand why they'd stopped. Lifting one paw she scratched at the gate.

Mandy grimaced and gritted her teeth. 'Shh!'

The collie studied the worn wooden barrier between them and her puppy and shook her tousled head. 'Yap!' She gave a loud, sharp bark.

With their nerves already on edge, Mandy and James jumped out of their skins. Henrietta strained at her lead and scrabbled at the gate. Blackie joined in the fun. Now there was no chance that the fox would be allowed to go on eating in peace. 'We'd better take a look,' James sighed.

So they stood on tiptoe to peer over the tall gate, expecting to see a flash of a bushy red tail, a white tip, as the fox stole back into the safety of the stable. 'Can you see anything?' Mandy whispered.

James shook his head. 'Here, I'll give you a hitch up, Mandy.' He knelt and cupped his hands, waiting for her to step on to the support and clutch the top of the gate.

To do this, Mandy had to let go of Henrietta's

lead. 'Stay!' she hissed, without much hope that the dog would obey. Soon though, she was clinging to the gate and peering into the yard.

She gasped. 'I don't believe it!'

'What?' James's arms sagged and gave way under her weight. He left her hanging from the top of the gate.

Then Mandy's own arms weakened. She dropped to the ground. 'James, you're not going to believe this either!'

'What?' His eyes were wide and insistent. Blackie was still scrabbling at the gate, and Henrietta had begun to bounce up at it too. Its old hinges creaked, the latch rattled.

As if in answer to his question, while Mandy still caught her breath and shook her head in disbelief, the rusty latch gave way. The gates swung open.

And now both Mandy and James could see clearly across the yard to the ramshackle area where Mrs Ponsonby kept her row of old metal dustbins. Instead of catching a glimpse of the bush-tailed fox slinking off to her hideaway in the stable, they saw the real villain, nose still buried in the litter of paper, peel and cans. Her tail wasn't long, her face not pointed, but flat, with a tiny snub nose. Her short legs waded through the waste paper and one front paw was neatly bandaged.

'Pandora!' James's eyes almost shot out of his head.

The little Pekinese dog was concentrating so hard on gobbling the contents of the dustbin that she didn't even notice her new audience. She snuffled and snaffled, teased at a gnawed chicken bone, then tossed it in the air. Then she burrowed her head into the upturned bin and waggled her feathery tail as she discovered the next treasure.

Mandy and James stood in shocked surprise, while Blackie and Henrietta ventured through the gate. For a second, everything was quiet, then chaos broke out.

'Woof!' Toby bounded out of the house into the yard.

'Blackie, stay!' James gasped.

The black Labrador charged at Toby and greeted him as a long lost friend.

'Woof, woof!' Toby ducked and wove. He bounded towards Henrietta.

The rough collie leaped into action. Like a giant doormat, she flung herself at Toby. They met in midair and rolled to the ground, a mass of fur, legs and tails. Blackie whirled round them, barking with all his might.

'It's OK, they're only playing,' Mandy said. Toby was delirious with joy to find new playmates in his yard. Meanwhile Pandora guzzled her way through a half-eaten pork pie.

But the noise brought Mrs Ponsonby rushing to the door. She was dressed in a tweed skirt and lilac jumper, long strings of pearls swinging across her ample bosom. On her feet she wore furry purple slippers.

The owner of Bleakfell Hall seized a broom that stood by the door. She wielded it like a knight holding his spear and charging into battle. 'Shoo, you horrid dogs!' she cried, her face red, her eyes glittering behind her gold-rimmed reading-glasses. 'Leave my poor Toby alone. Go on, shoo!'

Mandy glanced at the upturned bin. Pandora had moved on from pork pie to a greasy margarine tub, oblivious of the row going on in the yard. And now Mandy's own eyes gleamed. *This is my chance*! she thought.

'Hang on,' James warned, seeing what she was about to do. 'Let's just think about this first!'

But Mandy knew it was their golden opportunity to prove Mrs Ponsonby wrong about the fox. She

stepped forward and laid her hand on the arm that wielded the broom. 'Er, Mrs Ponsonby, would you just calm down a minute, please?'

'Shoo!' the old lady cried in a voice like a foghorn. She shook Mandy off.

'Would you please look at Pandora?' Mandy came back at her as Mrs Ponsonby bore down on the trio of playful dogs.

'Not now, dear. Can't you see I'm busy?'

'But I think you'd like to know what she's up to,' Mandy insisted, intent on getting their fox off the hook. All that was visible was Pandora's tubby little backside and feathery tail. The rest of her had disappeared deep inside the upturned bin. 'It's not the fox who's been raiding your dustbin. It's Pandora!'

Mrs Ponsonby stopped in mid-stride. Her broom-arm quivered, her jaw dropped. Then she swivelled round, following the direction of Mandy's pointing finger.

'What nonsense!' she began, refusing to believe the evidence of her own eyes.

'But it's true!' Mandy ran across to ease Pandora away from her grubby feast. Instead, the Pekinese squirmed further into the bin and out of sight.

Mrs Ponsonby shook her head. 'You're making it up. And look, these dogs of yours are completely out of control!' Once more she began to jab with her broom at Blackie and Henrietta.

Mandy was down on her hands and knees, struggling to extricate Pandora, James was tugging at Blackie, and Mrs Ponsonby was still parrying, when suddenly Henrietta broke away. The rough collie seemed to remember why they'd come here in the first place. She raced across the yard to the stables, running excitedly up and down, then pausing outside the stable where Nipper was hiding. She yelped and barked, sniffed at the door, then barked again. From inside the stable they heard a high, excited reply.

'Yap-yap. Yap-yap!'

'What was that?' All of a sudden, Mrs Ponsonby's eyes and ears were razor-sharp. 'Inside the stable; did you hear it?'

Blushing bright red, James shook his head. Mandy crawled out of the dustbin and got to her feet. 'Pandora's the one who's been stealing food from the bin!' she said, desperate to draw Mrs Ponsonby's attention away from the stable. But Henrietta was mad with joy at the sound of her pup's voice. She barked and waited for another reply. From inside the dark stable, Nipper barked back.

'You see, that's how she hurt her foot,' Mandy jabbered, following Mrs Ponsonby across the yard. 'Pandora must have cut it on an open can. It's obvious, isn't it?'

But Mrs Ponsonby could move quickly when she wanted to, and nothing Mandy could say would stop her. She was already at the stable door, lifting the latch . . . opening it.

'Oh!' Mrs Ponsonby stopped on the threshold. Mandy and James came up behind. They peered in together.

There was Sophie Dixon standing silently in the gloom. Her dark eyes flashed with anger as she stared out at Mandy, ignoring Mrs Ponsonby's gasp of shocked surprise. In her arms she held an excited puppy who barked and yelped as the light flooded in and he sensed his own mother. Henrietta had come to rescue him at last!

Nine

'It's not what you think!' Mandy told Sophie. She knew it looked as if she'd broken her promise and told Mrs Ponsonby about the intruders in her stable.

Sophie looked at her with disgust. 'You lied to me!'

'We didn't. You have to believe me!' Mandy gave up trying to hold on to Henrietta. She let the dog off the lead and watched as Sophie put the pup on the floor. Henrietta licked and nudged him, checking him from head to foot. Their tails wagged and they gave little yelps of pleasure.

'It's true.' James added his voice. 'We only came

to try and persuade you to take Nipper back home.'
He spread his hands in a helpless gesture. 'But
then it all went wrong.'

'Save your breath.' Sophie glowered at them.
'I don't even want to hear.' There were tears
in her eyes as she stooped to stroke Henrietta
and her puppy.

'Excuse me a moment.' Mrs Ponsonby found
her voice at last. 'This all seems very strange!' She
looked from Sophie to the two collies, then at
James and Mandy. 'Apparently everyone knows
what's going on here except me.'

'No, Sophie's making a mistake,' Mandy began,
still desperately trying to explain. 'She's got it
all wrong.'

But the angry girl flared up again. 'It's not me,
it's you. You broke your promise and now I'm going
to break mine!' She scooped Nipper into her arms
again and went up to a bewildered Mrs Ponsonby.
'Did you know you've got a fox living in this
stable?' she demanded. 'It's in the loft right now.
I saw it go up with my own eyes!'

Mrs Ponsonby gasped and took a step back.
'A fox?' she echoed. 'Actually here in my stable?
Is this true?' She turned to Mandy with a look
of horror.

Sophie's eyes glinted with spiteful triumph. 'I can prove it to you if you like.'

But before she had chance to take out her torch and shine it towards the dark loft, Mrs Ponsonby had decided to believe her and panic had set in. 'Toby, Pandora, come here at once!' she cried. 'Help me, Mandy. And James, get hold of Blackie. We have to get these dogs out of here before the fox decides to attack!'

'She's probably more scared of us than we are of her,' Mandy objected. At that moment she hated Sophie Dixon. Amidst all the noise and confusion, she pictured the poor fox cowering in a corner, her safe hiding-place stolen from her by Sophie's betrayal.

'Don't argue, dear. That's right, keep hold of Toby. I've got Pandora. Now, let's get them out into the yard.' She bustled ahead, only pausing once she was out in the fresh air to turn and make sure that Mandy and James were following. 'Is everyone safe? Where's the girl from the vicarage?'

With Toby squirming in her arms, Mandy glanced over her shoulder, expecting Sophie to be coming after them with Henrietta and Nipper. But there was no sign of her. Instead, the stable door swung open. There were fresh scuff marks in the frost, and messy footprints leading towards the gate.

'She must have slipped away with the dogs,' James muttered. 'A good job too.' He was as angry and disappointed as Mandy.

'Never mind now. I'll telephone her parents later on. What we must do first and foremost is deal with this fox!' Mrs Ponsonby had got over her panic and begun to assume command once more. 'I simply can't have the vicious thing taking refuge in there on a permanent basis. Goodness knows what damage it will do!'

Mandy recognised the tone of voice. There wasn't the least point trying to argue. *Wait*! she wanted to say. *Where will the fox go if you drive her out of here*? The stable was her shelter from the winter cold. Wasn't it bad enough that she'd had to watch Sam Western and his men shoot her partner? Wouldn't it be the most cruel thing to send her on her way, out into the frost, all alone?

But she hung her head and remained silent as Mrs Ponsonby strode towards the house.

The large woman halted on the doorstep to glance at the capsized dustbin and trail of rubbish. 'It's too bad,' she tutted. She turned to Mandy and

James. 'This may seem cruel, and I know it's going back on what I said yesterday about not needing guns, but that was before I knew that the fox had actually come to live in my back yard!'

'Oh no, please!' Mandy cried. 'You're not going to bring Mr Western back!'

For a moment Mrs Ponsonby hesitated. But then she shook herself and squared her shoulders. 'I'm sorry, Mandy,' she said at last. 'I'm not a violent person by nature, believe me. But you must see that I really have no alternative!'

As the stout figure of Mrs Ponsonby disappeared through the door, Mandy and James sprang into action.

'We're not going to stand by and let this happen!' she declared. They'd saved the vixen from Mr Western before, and they would do it again.

'Come on, we'd better be quick!' he agreed.

Telling Blackie to stay in the yard, they ran back to the stable.

Mandy was the first to reach the ancient ladder leading to the loft, and she began to clamber up it, explaining what she thought they should do. 'If we can get the fox away from here before anyone comes, at least she'll still have a chance!'

'Whereas if we just leave her, the Fox Watch lot will be here, and Mr Western with his gun as well.' James too had spotted the ruthless note in Mrs Ponsonby's voice. 'Where is she, Mandy? Can you see her?' He dragged himself on to the high wooden platform after her.

'Not yet.' She peered into the pitch blackness, just able to make out bundles of straw and old hay bales piled haphazardly in one corner. 'You know, we've only got Sophie's word that she's still up here!'

James took a deep breath. 'Yes, but I can smell her. That means she's been here recently, even if she's not here now.'

'You reckon she'll come back in any case?'

He nodded. Then he dropped on to one knee and pushed some straw to one side. He picked up a small bone, picked clean of meat. 'Look at this.'

Mandy crouched to study the chicken bone. The fox must have scavenged it from the dustbin. And it was true, the smell of the fox was still strong and bitter. She would almost have said it was a hot smell. 'I think she is still here!'

They listened. But there wasn't much time. Soon Mrs Ponsonby would have made her phone calls and would be rushing back to take charge.

'Let's try the far corner,' Mandy said. She pointed to the untidy stack of bales. 'If she's up here, that's the most likely place for her to be hiding.'

'I'll prop the door open so she can run straight out.' James saw that it had swung shut since they'd climbed up to the loft. He went back to the ladder and began to climb down.

So Mandy crept forward alone on her hands and knees, under the low eaves of the stable roof. 'I'm very sorry,' she murmured. 'I know it looks as if we're driving you away, but it's for your own good!' If the vixen was hiding nearby, she hoped that a gentle voice would calm her.

She heard a rustle in the straw, then a faint whicker. Instinctively Mandy froze, hunched close to the floor, one hand on the nearest bale.

There was another movement, and then a glint in the darkest corner of the loft. A pair of amber eyes stared.

Mandy held her breath. Now she could make out the whole face of the fox. She saw that the vixen was smaller and her head narrower than the dog fox that had been killed. She too was crouched, head down, her pointed ears twitching, waiting for Mandy to make the next move.

In spite of the danger the fox was in, in spite of Mrs Ponsonby's panic and Sophie Dixon's meanness, for a moment Mandy was spellbound. She forgot everything except for the quick, clever beauty of the animal; her sharp face bordered with white, her black nose and those deep gold, cat-like eyes.

'Is she there?' James called from below.

His voice triggered the fox into action. Her ears flicked and there was a swish from her long, bushy tail. Then she opened her long mouth and flattened her ears. Her teeth were white and pointed; dangerous sharp spikes for holding on to her struggling prey.

But Mandy didn't back off. 'Yes,' she called back. 'I'm going to try to drive her down the ladder. Can you make sure she gets out of the door before Mrs Ponsonby shows up?'

'I'll do my best. But hurry up, I think I just heard her come back into the yard!'

So Mandy made a crude lunge at the fox, intended to scare her out of the corner and down the ladder. The sudden, clumsy movement worked, for the vixen darted forward. In one lithe bound she cleared Mandy's crouching figure.

'Watch out, here she comes!' she called, whirling

round to follow the fox's progress.

'I see her!' James held the door wide open.

But the russet-brown shape raced along the length of the loft, away from the ladder.

Mandy's heart sank. 'This way!' she pleaded. At this rate, they would be too late. Mrs Ponsonby would trap her again, Mr Western would turn up, and all would be lost.

It seemed as if the clever animal understood that she had to get out. But she would do it her own way. When she reached the far end, she stopped and took a quick look over the edge, as if measuring the distance to the floor below. *No ladder for me!* she seemed to say. She sat back on her haunches and launched herself into midair in a flurry of straw. In a split second she had landed safely, sprinted for the door and vanished.

'Thank heavens!' Mandy stood up and brushed herself down. She joined James at the door as Mrs Ponsonby caught sight of the fleeing fox.

'Pandora, Toby! Heel!' she screeched.

James raised her eyebrows and shook his head. Mandy shrugged. The last thing on the poor fox's mind was stopping to scrap with Mrs Ponsonby's dogs. She sped across the yard, past the dustbins and round the side of the house; a lean streak of rusty red, with a white flash of tail.

'Oh dear!' Mrs Ponsonby was red and flustered. 'I promised Sam Western that I would keep the fox locked inside the stable! He's already on his way down from Upper Welford Hall. Mandy, dear, what happened? How did it escape?'

'She was too fast for us,' Mandy mumbled, glad that Mrs Ponsonby had a thousand and one things on her mind.

'. . . And I rang the Dixons to tell them that their daughter had been secretly hiding a puppy in my stable, and they said they'd come straight over, even though I tried to tell them that Sophie had already made herself scarce . . .'

'Well, we'd best be on our way too,' Mandy suggested. She didn't fancy being at Bleakfell Hall when any of these people arrived.

But Mrs Ponsonby caught her by the wrist. '. . . That's not all.' Finally I telephoned Animal Ark with my suspicions that you and James were tangled up in this situation, so your father is on his way, too! He asked me to tell you to stay where you were until he got here.'

Mandy groaned and sagged.

'Not that I understand anything about what's been going on.' Plump Mrs Ponsonby looked and sounded out of her depth. 'Why would Sophie Dixon need to hide that sweet little puppy in my draughty old stable?'

'Because nobody wanted him and she's afraid that her parents would want to have him put down,' Mandy confessed quietly.

'Not want him? Have him put to sleep?' The colour drained from Mrs Ponsonby's face. 'Whatever for?'

'Because he can't see very well,' James explained. 'There's something wrong with his eyes.'

'You mean he's short-sighted?'

He nodded. 'Something like that. It's called collie eye.'

Mrs Ponsonby took time to consider this. She drew a deep breath and her bosom swelled. 'Well, I can't see so well myself, but I hope nobody is considering having *me* put down!' She began to tut. Pacing up and down the yard, she took in the news that Mandy and James had just given her. 'I know that not everybody adores dogs as much as we do, Mandy dear, but I would never have thought that a little vision problem is any reason for putting a puppy to sleep! And now I've made a mess of things by phoning the Dixons, haven't I?'

Mandy forgave her the moment she saw how

much Mrs Ponsonby regretted what she'd done. She went to pace alongside her. 'Can't we stop them somehow?'

'How? Oh, Mandy, and it's nearly Christmas, a time of joy and good cheer! We should all be looking forward to it. But how can we celebrate with this great shadow hanging over that poor puppy's head? Oh dear!'

'Not to mention the poor fox,' Mandy murmured. But Mrs Ponsonby was far too caught up in her worries about Nipper to hear her.

'Here comes a car,' James warned, going round the side of the house to look. 'I think it's the Dixons!'

And sure enough, by the time Mandy and Mrs Ponsonby had joined him, with Pandora, Toby and Blackie running excitedly between their legs, the big Range Rover had crunched to a halt in the front drive.

The tall, stern figure of Andrew Dixon jumped out first, slamming the driver's door behind him. Then Helena Dixon stepped down, her face serious as she held open the passenger door.

'Sophie!' Mandy gasped, as the Dixon's daughter appeared. She was white and trembling, her dark hair falling across her face. Her jeans were torn on one knee, her shoes muddy. She left Henrietta in the back seat of the Range Rover, but in her arms she held the tiny, half-blind pup.

'What? . . . How? . . .' For once Mrs Ponsonby was lost for words.

'We found them in the village, just about to get on a bus to Walton,' Mr Dixon told her. 'The bus driver didn't want to let Sophie on board with Henrietta and the puppy because they were so muddy.'

'Chasing across fields and goodness knows what,' Mrs Dixon put in. As usual, she looked immaculate in her tailored jacket and trousers.

Andrew Dixon took up the story again. 'We received your phone call, Mrs Ponsonby, and headed straight here. We passed by the bus stop just at the right moment. It seems Sophie's got an awful lot of explaining to do.' He spoke quietly, as if he was trying to make up his mind about what was going on.

'Yes, and I don't see how she's going to come up with a good reason for what she's done.' Helena Dixon couldn't hide her disapproval. 'She told us the puppy was lost, but it seems she's been lying to us right from the start!'

'It wasn't Sophie's fault.' Mandy tried to help.

She felt James tug at her jacket and saw his look of surprise. 'Well, it wasn't! She only brought Nipper here and hid him because she wanted to save his life!' Much as she hated Sophie for giving the whereabouts of their fox away, she still had to give credit where it was due.

Mr Dixon frowned, while his wife took him to one side. She whispered a hasty explanation. 'The puppy is half blind. I told Sophie it would be better to have him put down.'

'You might have informed me first,' he said, folding his arms and glancing at Nipper.

'I did, Andrew. But you must have been too busy to listen. You left me to make the decision, as usual. And now I'm the one who plays the baddie, just because it happens not to be what Sophie wants.'

'Hmm.' He scratched his chin and stared at his daughter.

Mandy bit her lip. This was like waiting for a verdict in court. Would Mr Dixon side with his wife or his daughter?

Then Mrs Ponsonby stepped in. 'Never mind all that now. What's past is past. I have an idea!' She had to raise her voice above the sound of another car as it approached along her drive.

Out of the corner of her eye Mandy saw the

Animal Ark Land-rover arrive. But instead of going to greet her dad, she stayed glued to the spot to hear Mrs Ponsonby's announcement.

'Let *me* take the puppy!' She strode over to Sophie and seized Nipper from her. 'He's adorable. It makes no different to me what his eyesight is like. He could be completely blind for all I care! I still think he's the most beautiful little chap! Yes, I do!' She held him up in both hands and wiggled him gently back and forth.

Mandy gasped. A home for Nipper out of the blue, from the very last person she would have expected!

'But . . .' Helena Dixon drew back her head in astonishment.

Her husband kept his eyes on Sophie, whose shoulders slumped as she slowly turned away and wandered towards their car.

'No, I won't hear any objections!' Mrs Ponsonby rattled on. 'I insist on giving a puppy a home here at Bleakfell Hall. We can't hear of him being put to sleep, can we, Pandora? Can we, Toby?' She cooed and dandled the puppy in front of them to let them all make friends.

By this time Adam Hope had joined the group. 'It might not be quite that simple,' he warned. 'If

a pup has collie eye, he can be much more difficult to train.'

Mandy frowned. Straight away she saw what he was getting at. Mrs Ponsonby might not have enough patience or even common sense to look after a special puppy like Nipper. After all neither of her dogs was particularly well-behaved.

Mrs Ponsonby gave him a beaming smile. 'Nonsense, Adam. You're talking to a dog expert, you know!'

'Yes, but, Mrs Ponsonby . . .' He tried again.

'*Amelia*!' she reminded him.

Mandy saw her dad blush to the roots of his hair. She followed the argument, turning her head from one to the other like a spectator at a tennis match. On the one hand, any home for the puppy was better than none. On the other, she trusted her dad's opinion, and it was obvious that he didn't think that Mrs Ponsonby had come up with a very good answer to the problem.

'. . . Amelia,' he stammered. 'Have you considered how Pandora and Toby would adjust to living with a partially-sighted dog? They're used to having your attention all to themselves, you know.'

'What are you suggesting, Adam? That I spoil

my dogs?' Mrs Ponsonby's voice rose an octave.

'Not at all . . . er, Amelia. I just want to point out the pitfalls.'

'Nonsense, nonsense!' She waved away his objections and turned back to the owners. 'Now, Mr and Mrs Dixon, it's up to you. What do you say?'

Ten

'I'm not sure.' Andrew Dixon looked to Adam Hope. 'You're the expert. What do you think?'

Mandy and James hardly dared to move. Nipper's life hung by a thread.

'Come now, Adam, you think it's the perfect answer, don't you?' Mrs Ponsonby was so involved in the brilliance of her solution that she failed to notice yet another car swing through her gates.

'Well . . .' Mandy's dad was just beginning to see the implications of his advice. 'Don't look at me like that!' he whispered at Mandy as Mrs Ponsonby dandled the puppy and cooed into his furry brown-and-white face. In the Dixons' Range

Rover, Sophie sat huddled, staring blankly at the hills behind Bleakfell Hall.

'Like what?' Mandy tried to hide her fears. But she knew she was biting her lip hard and digging her fingernails into the palms of her hands.

'Like I'm handing down a death sentence,' Mr Hope murmured, glad that Mrs Ponsonby's attention had been diverted by the arrival of Sam Western and Dennis Saville. 'What do *you* think we should do?'

'Let Mrs Ponsonby keep Nipper?' she sighed. Sometimes a decision was too difficult for her ever to be sure.

But then, crises piled on top of one another. Before Adam Hope had delivered a verdict on Nipper, Mandy saw the hard look set into the lines on Mr Western's face as he jumped down from his car and slammed the door. She saw the shotgun under his arm, and the muscular brown-and-black shape of Major trotting at his heels. Behind the landowner and his dog came the farm manager, Dennis Saville. He too carried a gun.

'I hear you have an unwelcome guest in your stable,' Mr Western said to Mrs Ponsonby. He had no time for pleasantries. 'And I understand you don't want any more shilly-shallying. Well, I'm glad to hear it.' His voice was gruff, and he ignored the Dixons, Mr Hope, Mandy and James. There was serious business to be done.

'Yes, it's true.' Mrs Ponsonby still clutched Nipper as she went to confer with Mr Western. 'It gave me a terrible shock when I heard. Apparently, not only has it been raiding my bins, but it's chosen my hayloft as its winter lodgings!'

'Well, leave it to us this time. Dennis and I will deal with it.' He gestured for his manager to follow him across the yard.

Mandy and James stood between the two men and the stables. For a moment, Mandy set her mind against stepping out of the way. She glared into their faces, aware of the dull grey metal of their guns, the curved triggers and long thin barrels. But she knew they were wasting their time if they thought they could stride into the stables and make their kill. All they would find would be musty straw, an empty loft, and the sharp smell that the fox had left behind.

So she stood to one side, and felt James step in the other direction. Western and Saville pushed through the middle, ignoring Mrs Ponsonby's hurried explanation until they reached the stable door.

'It's not quite that simple, Mr Western. The fox was there until a few minutes ago, but I'm afraid it's not there now.'

'Not here?' Sam Western's frown deepened as he stopped in his tracks. 'But I thought you said . . .'

Mandy saw the colour rise in Mrs Ponsonby's cheeks. Perhaps she was regretting calling Mr Western after all.

'It escaped.' The large lady's voice faltered. 'In any case, I'm still not one hundred percent sure that I want to have it destroyed.'

Mr Western snorted and pushed at the stable door. 'You prefer to have it prowling round your yard for the rest of the winter, do you?'

'Of course not. But I should have consulted with the other members of my Fox Watch scheme before I did anything hasty.'

It was Dennis Saville's turn to grunt and dismiss her protest. 'Just stand clear, Mrs Ponsonby. Let us check for his scent and see if we can pick up his trail.'

'*Her* trail!' Mandy said, glaring at the two men. 'You *shot* the dog fox, remember!'

As the door swung open on the empty stable, Mr Western glanced at her. 'I don't suppose you and your friend here could have had anything to do with this so-called "escape"?'

Mandy's chin went up. She stood shoulder to shoulder with James.

'Oh, never mind,' Western grunted. 'Come on, Dennis, the sooner we get after this fox the better.'

With Mrs Ponsonby fussing behind them, and Mandy's dad talking quietly to the Dixons, Mandy and James watched the landowner and his man shove their way into the gloomy stable. 'Let's hope we gave her a good enough start,' James whispered.

Mandy nodded. 'She's clever. She'd cover her tracks.' She remembered what her dad had said about the wiliness of foxes.

But still they held their breaths and waited, listening to the two men poking at the straw inside the stable and muttering to each other.

'It's no good looking in there!' a voice said, loud and clear.

Mandy turned to see Sophie Dixon standing right behind them.

At the sound of her voice, Mr Western came out. He brushed straw from his jacket, then shouldered his gun. 'What's that?'

'I said it's no good looking for the fox in there. You won't find her.' Sophie spoke as if she knew something important, in that secretive way she had, ignoring Mandy and James and staring at Mr Western.

'Have you got a better idea?' he demanded.

Sophie nodded. She stood with her hands in her pockets, in her mud-covered jeans, determined to have her say. 'I saw which way she went.'

Mandy narrowed her eyes. *Don't you dare*! She put all her strength of will into defying Sophie. But it made no difference.

'Good. That's more like it.' Western called Saville out of the stable. 'This girl's got the information we need.'

'How? When?' James challenged. 'You weren't here!'

'That's right. Don't listen to her!' Mandy agreed. How could Sophie Dixon do this to a poor defenceless creature?

'I didn't have to be,' she sneered. 'I didn't see her here, did I? I saw her in the village!'

Mandy could have strangled her. She felt her face go hot with anger and then cold with dismay. For the second time in two days Sophie had betrayed their fox.

'Whereabouts?' Immediately Western took up the clue. 'Where exactly did you see her?' He gestured at Saville to go ahead and start up the car engine.

'I was at the bus-stop by the post office. The fox was sneaking along the back of those little houses next to the pub.'

'That's Ernie Bell's place. Which way was it heading?'

Sophie narrowed her eyes. She shot a look at Mandy, warning her not to interfere.

Mandy picked up the look. Somehow it wasn't the expression an enemy would give. *Keep quiet*! it signalled. *Trust me!*

'Which way?' Mr Western demanded again.

'Towards the village hall.'

'Crossing the main road?' For a second he looked doubtful. 'In broad daylight?'

'Yes, but then it cut back behind the houses and went into the pub yard. Behind that high wall.'

'Then what?' He squeezed every drop of information he could out of his willing helper.

'Then the bus came, so I don't know where it went after that. But I think it must have found something to eat in the dustbins behind the pub, don't you?' She sounded eager, nodding her head in encouragement.

'Quite likely.' Sam Western nodded hastily back. 'That's a big help, thank you very much!'

With this, he strode across Mrs Ponsonby's yard

and into his Land-rover. He'd heard all he needed. Now it was time for action.

James waited until the car turned and set off down the drive, then he grabbed Mandy's arm. 'Come on, what are we waiting for?' he cried.

The grown-ups had gone into a huddle, while the dogs trotted quietly round the yard. Mrs Ponsonby kept tight hold of little Nipper and was anxiously discussing the recent turn of events.

'Come on, Mandy!' James insisted. 'We're not going to give up now, are we?' He was all for cutting across the fields to get to the village before Mr Western.

But Mandy stood firm. She was waiting for Sophie to say something. 'That wasn't true, was it?' she murmured.

Sophie's pale face blushed. 'I was afraid you two were going to ruin it!'

'How come?' James was puzzled. 'Ruin what?'

'There I was, trying my best to make them believe what I was saying, and you were telling them not to believe me!'

'You mean it wasn't true?' James was flabbergasted. He watched Sam Western's car turn left out of the gates and speed towards the village. 'You didn't see the fox?'

'Yes, I did.' Sophie's eyes were beginning to gleam. 'But not exactly where I said I did!'

'Wow!' His mouth fell open.

Mandy heaved a sigh of relief. 'You sent them the wrong way?'

She nodded. 'It's a good job you picked up what I was trying to do, Mandy.'

'I wasn't sure . . .'

'No, and I wouldn't have blamed you for not trusting me, after what I've done.' Again Sophie blushed. 'I was just so worried about Nipper, I couldn't think straight.'

'Never mind that now.' Mandy spoke gently. 'Listen, at least Nipper won't have to be put down if Mrs Ponsonby has him.' She glanced across at the lively discussion going on amongst the adults. 'I know it's not perfect, but . . .'

'It's better than nothing,' Sophie agreed with a sigh. 'I just love that puppy so much, I don't know if I can bear to part with him!' Tears filled her eyes, and she wiped them away with the cuffs of her jacket.

'I'm sorry,' Mandy whispered.

'What for? It should be me who's saying sorry to you. I've ruined things for your fox, haven't I?'

'No. I should have seen how hard it was for you. But I never stopped to think.'

'None of us did,' James cut in. 'The thing is, Sophie, if you did see the fox and it wasn't by the pub, where was it?' Practical things suited him better than saying sorry.

For the first time they saw Sophie Dixon smile. The corners of her mouth curled and she shook her dark hair back from her face. 'Where do you think?'

'Don't make us guess!' James protested.

But Mandy grinned back. 'No, wait a minute.' She thought of their last sight of the vixen; the leap down from the loft on to the stable floor, the flesh of her white tail as she sped across the yard and round the side of the house.

'Where's the best place she'd found in the whole of Welford?' Sophie prompted.

'Here.' Mandy looked around the yard at the upturned bins, the deserted stables of Bleakfell Hall. 'You don't mean . . . ?'

'. . . She turned tail and came back home!' James finished the sentence for her.

Sophie admitted that she'd seen the fox return while she sat in the car watching everyone argue over Nipper. The fox had slunk back down the side of the house, across the yard and into the stable.

'You mean, she's in there now?' Adam Hope picked up the threads of the story as Mandy gave a high-speed account.

'Oh, Sophie!' Helena Dixon began to chide.

But Mandy's dad put up his hand to stop her. 'No, she just saved a life. Please don't tell her off.'

'But she lied.' Sophie's mother was embarrassed.

'Well, maybe a white lie doesn't come amiss when it's in a good cause. As a vet, I'm all for anything that protects the wildlife in the area, believe me!'

Mandy and James nodded hard, noticing Mrs Ponsonby's head go to one side as she listened and considered his opinion.

'Oh really, Adam? You see saving the fox as a question of protecting our natural heritage?'

'I certainly do, Amelia.'

Mandy grinned at James and Sophie.

'Yes, I see your point. Conservation work. Perhaps that's the way for our Fox Watch scheme to look at it too.'

'Exactly!' Adam Hope winked at Mandy. 'And very important work it is, too.'

'Hmm. "Save Our Foxes!" I like the sound of that.'

' "Fight for Foxes!" ' Andrew Dixon suggested. 'We could certainly get something going in the neighbourhood along those lines!'

Sophie and Helena Dixon stared at him in surprise.

'We could enlist some help too.' Mr Dixon sounded enthusiastic. 'I'm sure Joe would broadcast the message tomorrow night if we were to ask him. The whole village will be there to watch him turn on the lights, won't they?'

'Excellent!' Mrs Ponsonby squeezed Nipper and lent her weight to the new idea. 'Perhaps we could even get him to introduce a new storyline into Dale End. You know; a local widow who offers refuge to some starving foxes when a landowner turfs them off his property!'

'Who knows?' Mr Dixon disguised a smile. 'We can certainly try.'

'But meanwhile, back to reality,' Adam Hope reminded them. 'According to Sophie, we have a fox holed up in your stable, Mrs Pon – er, Amelia. And it seems she's chosen it as a safe bolthole for the winter. If I tell you that she will present absolutely no threat to Toby and Pandora, we can take it you have no objections to her staying here?'

Mrs Ponsonby drew herself up and took a deep breath. 'Absolutely none at all, my dear Adam!'

So while the others went into the house to celebrate over sherry and mince-pies, Adam Hope took a piece of cooked chicken from Mrs Ponsonby's fridge and went with Mandy and James into the stable. They wanted to reassure themselves that the fox had come to no harm after her recent adventures.

'Don't worry, foxes are talented survivors,' Mr Hope told them as they climbed the ladder to the loft. 'And they're brilliant opportunists.'

'Meaning what?' Mandy showed him the corner where the vixen had first chosen to hide.

'When they see a chance, they seize it. I'm not surprised that she made her way back here as soon as ever she could. After all, it's the warmest, driest place around.' He stopped to look behind the pile of bales. 'Yep, she's back all right.'

Mandy listened. In the darkness, as her senses grew used to the gloomy stable, and she breathed in the musty, disused smell, she too could her the soft, dog-like panting of the fox. 'Give her the chicken, Dad,' she whispered.

Adam Hope laid the bait, stood back and waited

for the vixen to emerge. At last they saw the glow of her eyes, then the white of her muzzle and chest, as the scent of chicken drew her out from behind the bales. They watched her take one low, delicate step, then another, her black paws invisible in the dim light. She kept them fully in her sights as she came warily forward.

'She looks OK,' Adam Hope said, casting his expert eye over her rich, thick coat. 'No damage done, I should say.'

'Thank goodness.' Mandy was smiling now, admiring the cheek of the vixen as she seized the piece of chicken and stared directly at them.

'That's your Christmas dinner,' James told her.

They all grinned. 'Do you want the other good news?' Mr Hope asked.

'Yes, please.' They took what they knew would be their last view of the fox in her luxury den. After this, they must leave her in peace to fend for herself and live a natural life in the wild.

'It looks like she's pregnant. In March or April she should be having a litter of three or four healthy cubs.'

Mandy sighed. 'That's brilliant!'

'Perfect!' James agreed.

Eleven

'Ladies and gentlemen, I take great pleasure in wishing you a very merry Christmas!'

Mandy watched as Joe Wortley stepped up on to a platform, flicked a switch and turned on the lights.

People cheered and clapped. The village square winked red and green, orange and blue. The Christmas tree towered above them, carols played on a loudspeaker and the landlord of the Fox and Goose came round with big plates of free mince-pies.

Ernie Bell was right at the front. 'Merry Christmas, Mandy,' he said with a wink, taking a mince-pie.

There was Walter, chatting with Jean. Gran and Grandad stood in the middle of the crowd with Simon. And James had come with his mum and dad and Blackie, armed with his autograph book, standing in line for an autograph from the famous television star.

'By the way.' Joe Wortley took up the microphone once more. 'I've been asked to make a special announcement.' He glanced down at Mrs Ponsonby, who stood by the platform, beaming up at him. 'This is on behalf of Amelia Ponsonby, who would like to invite you all to a party at Bleakfell Hall on Boxing Day afternoon.

'As you know, Amelia has just set up a new conservation group called Fox Watch, dedicated to the protection of one of our finest local inhabitants, *Vulpes vulpes*, or the European Red Fox. The party is a fund-raising effort to support her group, and of course refreshments of a seasonal nature will be provided. She very much hopes you'll all come!'

'Will you be there, Joe?' someone called from the crowd.

The actor nodded. 'You bet,' he said, before putting down the microphone.

'Then we'll be there too,' the voice promised.

Mandy stood between her mum and dad, grinning as Mrs Ponsonby swamped Joe Wortley with thanks. Dressed for the occasion in her red coat and matching red Santa Claus hat, with Toby and Pandora at her feet, she radiated happiness.

'Good job Sam Western's not here to hear that,' Adam Hope said quietly. There'd be no news of the landowner since Sophie had sent him off on the wild-goose chase.

'Yes, but where's Nipper?' Mandy looked hard for him between the feet of the crowd surrounding Mrs Ponsonby and Joe Wortley. There was no sign of the puppy, yet Mandy couldn't imagine that his doting new owner would have left him behind.

'Here,' a voice said from behind.

Mandy turned. 'Sophie!'

'Yap!' Nipper greeted her from the safety of Sophie's arms.

'Woof!' Henrietta wasn't to be outdone. Her deep bark startled people nearby. She stared up at Mandy.

'But . . . !' Mandy looked from Sophie to Nipper to Henrietta. She glanced across at Mrs Ponsonby's red hat bobbing through the crowd towards them.

'Mum and Dad decided we could keep Nipper after all!' Sophie declared. 'Your dad helped to persuade them, Mandy. Thanks to him, Nipper can stay at the vicarage with Henrietta and me!'

'That's fantastic!' Mandy knew that Sophie deserved it. She would love him and care for him in a special way.

'Will you come and take them for walks with me?' Sophie asked shyly. 'You could help me to train Nipper if you like.'

'I'd love to!' Mandy was thrilled at how well everything had turned out. But Mrs Ponsonby was getting dangerously close. 'Listen, Sophie, I'll see you later, OK? I want to tell James your good news!'

She escaped in the nick of time, just before Mrs Ponsonby descended on Nipper.

'How's the sweet little darling?' Mandy heard the cooing voice rise above the carols. 'Has he missed me, then? I'm sure he has. But he's in a very good home, so there's no need to worry his sweet little head about anything. And he's going to have such a happy Christmas, I know he is!'

'Hey!' James cried as Mandy seized his arm. 'Where are we off to now?'

She pulled him away from the mince-pies and the singing, out of the laughing crowd.

'Escaping from Mrs Ponsonby,' she told him. 'Let's make a quick getaway!'

The frosty air nipped their faces and made their fingers and toes tingle as they circled round the back of the pub into the quiet of the fields and the dark hillside beyond. Mandy breathed in deeply and gazed up at the clear starlit sky. A full moon cast a silvery light on the frozen landscape.

'Look there!' James whispered, pointing up the hill to a clump of hawthorn bushes, outlined in black by the light of the moon.

All was still and silent. Then Mandy saw a movement. A lonely figure the size of a smallish dog loped through the trees on to the empty moor.

But it was no dog. The nose was too sharp, the ears too pointed. And though they could only see the silhouette, the long, bushy tail gave her away.

'It's our fox,' she murmured.

'*A* fox,' James said.

It was true, it could have been any fox setting out on its nightly excursion across the frost-covered hill. But in her heart, Mandy knew her; the low, lithe run, the silent tread.

'*Our* fox,' she repeated, watching with a low satisfied sigh as the fox finally melted into the dark.